Her Bill
Troul

MW00531864

Two Billionaire Brothers determined to marry off their grandsons...one's going to do it even from the grave using his last will and testament...

Because of his granddaddy's odd Will, Morgan needs a wife and Amber has a secret crush and owes him her life... but will she lose her heart in their "fake" marriage?

According to his granddaddy's Will billionaire resort tycoon, Morgan McCoy must marry if he wants to retain ownership of the resort division of McCoy Enterprises. Morgan isn't happy and heads to Hawaii for business and to figure out if he will find a temporary wife or walk away from everything he's worked so hard to build.

When her boss's personal assistant summons Amber Caldwell to Kauai to help with a resort acquisition, she didn't hesitate. She's had a secret crush on her boss since taking the job, but he doesn't even know she exists. Maybe this is her chance to at least get a little closer to him. She isn't expecting nearly drowning her first day in paradise or being rescued by her gorgeous boss.

And she certainly isn't expecting Morgan McCoy to ask her to marry him—but it's an offer she can't refuse. After all, she owes him for saving her life.

But will she lose her heart when their contract ends?

HER BILLIONAIRE COWBOY'S TROUBLE IN PARADISE

McCoy Billionaire Brothers, Book Three

HOPE MOORE

Her Billionaire Cowboy's Trouble in Paradise

Copyright © 2019 Hope Moore

CHAPTER ONE

Morgan McCoy stood on the cliffs near the McCoy Paradise Resort, looking out over the royal-blue water on the shores of Kauai, Hawaii. He needed to be here on business so he'd come immediately after the reading of his granddaddy's will stating the specifications J.D. McCoy had set up in order for Morgan to retain control of the massive McCoy Stonewall Hotel and Resort Division of McCoy Stonewall Enterprises. A division worth billions on its own.

The requirements were ridiculous.

His granddaddy—the stubborn, controlling old coot—knew he had Morgan by the throat. He knew Morgan had put too much of himself into this business to walk away.

Unlike before he'd taken control of the division when he had been prepared to walk, he wasn't willing to lose it all and start over now. He was too invested. And if he walked, then his brothers also would lose all stock in his division. They'd each had to protect their stock in their own divisions of McCoy Stonewall Enterprises for each other to retain theirs and now, he had to do the same.

There were also no escape clauses in the will. Oh, he'd had his lawyers go over every angle. No, he was stuck, his path decided—his granddaddy was probably laughing in his grave that he'd gotten the last say.

The wind and mist coming off the ocean and the lava rocks that formed the cliffs where he stood watching the turtles swimming in the waves crashing against the rocks slammed into Morgan, plastering his clothing to him and bringing him out of his brooding. The sky was a mixture of navy with pale streaks of baby blues struggling with the approaching gray clouds. A storm was brewing off the coast, stirring up the undercurrents. It would be a fierce night.

The view from his penthouse suite at the top of the

McCoy Paradise Resort would be a mighty show to watch. But right now, he needed to be near the water. It always helped calm him. Not so today. Instead, the fierce turmoil he could see in the approaching sky mimicked the turmoil inside him. He stared down, studying the rocks below him. He watched the sea turtles cavort in the turbulent waters, seeming to enjoy the rough ride they had among crashing waves and the massive lava rocks. It always amazed him that they weren't slammed to pieces against these rocks. Watching them always inspired him to keep fighting for what he wanted. To enjoy the sport of it and to never let himself get down or defeated.

And that's what he had always done, building his division of McCoy Stonewall Enterprises into the powerhouse it was.

And now his granddaddy had, with the flick of a pen, basically thrown him to the sharks.

If he didn't marry within three months, and stay married for three months, McCoy Stonewall Hotel and Resort Division would be sold to Lexington Industries, his number-one competitor, at rock-bottom prices. Everything he had worked for would be gone with the flourish of a lawyer's pen and his granddaddy's last will and testament.

Over the wind, he heard a shriek, probably a seagull. He glanced, searching the seagulls as it didn't exactly register as the usual shriek they made. Then the sound came again, drawing his gaze from the sky to the beach, then to the water. Offshore, he caught sight of thrashing arms. Someone was struggling.

Morgan's adrenaline shot up. He moved quickly across the massive lava rock, dodging the tide pool as he hurried to the edge then scrambled down the somewhat treacherous rocks toward the sand. When he'd reached a small enough distance that he could jump, he scanned the water to where he could still see the person who was in trouble. Then he leapt to the sand and hit the ground running.

He kept his eyes on the swimmer as he ran, his legs burning from the pace. He prayed he hadn't been too far away to reach the person in time. The person went under water again and Morgan dug deep, fought for more speed. He spotted the small head and arm resurface. Near enough now, he pounded into the water, stretched his arms forward, and dove hard into the waves. He hit the water, shooting through it, thankful in that moment that he had always been a strong swimmer. He surfaced, scanned the water where he thought the swimmer should be, and he saw a hand just as it disappeared beneath the surface.

He dove deep, pushed with all his might, keeping his eyes open. He spotted the dark mass of hair—*a woman*. He grabbed for her, snagged her arm, and wrapped an arm around her; then he kicked for the surface.

When he reached the surface, he sucked in air and glanced at the woman, who was unresponsive. Morgan swam hard for the shore. People had gathered and watched as he strode from the water and to the sand.

"We've called for help," a man called from the group.

He dropped to his knees and placed the woman on the sand. He immediately began efforts to resuscitate her. "Come on," he said between breaths. "Come on. Breathe." He leaned in to give her another breath of air when she twitched then coughed. "Yes, way to go." He rolled her to her side and held her as she coughed and the seawater came out.

"Move aside, move aside."

At the words, he looked over his shoulder and saw the EMTs hurrying toward him. His hope for the woman surged.

He moved to the side and let them take his place, telling them the details as they asked for them. Then he stood and moved out of their way. He watched from a few feet back, wondering what had happened. The woman was dark-headed, late twenties or early thirties. Pale as a ghost. And pretty, probably. But at the moment, she was so drained and coughing so hard it was really hard to tell. As he watched, he couldn't help wondering why she had gone out so far that she couldn't get back to safety.

"Do you know who this is? Are you with her?" the EMT asked as they loaded her onto the stretcher.

Morgan stared at her, getting the odd sense that he'd seen her before. "I'm not sure. I think I've seen her somewhere, maybe at the resort."

"Okay, we're going to take her in now."

"Where?"

"To Wilcox Medical in Lihue."

"I hate for her to go alone." He scanned the beach

6

but no one seemed to look as if they were with her. Everyone just looked like curious onlookers. Morgan felt hugely protective suddenly. He had saved her, after all. So why wouldn't he feel protective? "I'll come with you."

"I'm sorry, sir, but if you're not a relative, you can't get on the ambulance with her."

He followed beside them as they carried the gurney. Urgency filled him as they loaded her into the back of the ambulance. "You take care of her. I'll get my car and be there soon."

The EMT climbed in and grabbed the door. "That will be good. Just in case they have questions."

"I'll be there."

And then the doors closed and the ambulance headed out, siren blaring.

Morgan spun and, without hesitating, headed toward the resort.

Amber Rhodes woke to the sounds of bleeps and the smell of antiseptic. Confused, she looked around the hospital room. *What? How had she gotten here? What happened?* She stared at the IV in her arm and then looked at the machines that were hooked up to her. She glanced at her heart rate. It looked and felt inside her chest like it was beating just fine.

What had happened? Foggy memories tried to come into focus.

"Good. You're awake." A smiling, female nurse in blue hospital scrubs walked into the room. "*Howzit?*"

Amber felt a sense of relief at understanding that *howzit* was a Hawaiian greeting for *how are you?* "I've been better, thank you."

"I'm Luana and I'll be your nurse for the night."

"Luana, can you tell me how I got here? What happened?"

"In an ambulance. You cannot remember anything?" Luana was very pretty, with dark, straight hair and kind brown eyes that peered into Amber's eyes. Before Amber could find an answer, Luana placed her thumb on Amber's pulse and began counting as she looked at her watch.

Amber was impatient to figure out why she was here, trying to go through her memory to place what had happened. But it was so foggy. It wouldn't do any good while the nurse was checking her pulse.

When she finished, the nurse released her wrist. "So, do you remember anything?"

Amber remembered her name, remembered she worked for Morgan McCoy, but what else? "This was my first time in Kauai, or Hawaii for that matter. I went swimming. *Swimming*," she gasped as suddenly her terror of earlier filled her mind. "I went too far."

She was fumbling but that's what was at the edge of her fuzzy brain. Yes, she had worked for Morgan McCoy for a year. She was one of his executive assistant's assistants and had been called to Kauai at the last minute to help Mrs. Beasley.

The moment she'd gotten the call, Amber hadn't hesitated; she had packed her bag and jumped on the next flight out. Mr. McCoy and Mrs. Beasley had flown out the day before on a private jet. Morgan McCoy didn't fly with an entourage. He never had, as far as she knew. And she knew almost everything there was to know about the man. He fascinated her.

There were two reasons she had been excited about this trip, the first being that she would be closer to him and there was a slight possibility that he might actually notice her. In the office, surrounded by the chaos of their main offices, he had very limited interaction with anyone who wasn't on his direct personal team. His team members worked directly with him and those were the people who had access to him. Amber just watched him from afar. She was well aware that she had developed an unhealthy infatuation with her boss. But still, that knowledge hadn't lessened her excitement about coming on this trip.

The second reason she had been excited to be on the trip was that she had heard that the beautiful resort they owned in Kauai was especially amazing because the grounds were beautiful. Of course, Kauai was amazing in itself, a virtual paradise. So here she was, now on her first ever wonderful trip, and she was in the hospital with all kinds of things hooked up to her. Mrs. Beasley was going to be highly, highly upset.

"When can I get out? I'm here on business and I need to get back to my hotel and get ready to meet with my bosses in the morning."

"I'm sorry but you're going to have to remain here for observation. You took in a good bit of water. I don't think you realize how close you came to dying.

Thankfully, the man who saved you got to you before you drowned. You're very, very lucky to be alive. He happened to be on the lava cliffs beside the McCoy Paradise Resort in Poipu, the one where all of the beautiful sea turtles come in to dive and catch the waves. From his vantage point, he saw you and got to you in time."

A chill raced down her spine as memories of being caught in the undercurrent flashed through her mind. Amber wasn't sure what cliffs Luana was talking about because she had never been to the resort before. She had gone straight to her room, changed into her bathing suit, and immediately gone down to the beach. She wasn't sure when she would have a chance to do it again because Mrs. Beasley had told her to report for work the next morning. And when you worked for Morgan McCoy, you worked. And that was probably her last chance to immerse herself in the beautiful, beautiful water. She clearly had made a mistake.

"Someone saved me?" she asked, feeling slightly dimwitted, considering Luana had said exactly that. But Amber's brain was still fuzzy.

"Yes. He's actually outside, hoping to see you. He

was worried about you. What I heard through the hospital grapevine was that he tried to ride in the ambulance but they refused to let him."

"Really?"

"He's here—he came immediately. Although, I'm gathering from his clothing that he might have changed since he's not soaking wet."

Amber couldn't see her face but could only imagine what she looked like. Still, she needed to thank whoever this was who saved her life. "Please show him in. I need to thank him."

"I'll do that and I'll also let the doctors know you're awake."

Moments later, Amber nearly choked again on the sip of water she had been taking when none other than her boss, Morgan McCoy, strode through her hospital door.

"Hello," he said, his penetrating eyes taking her in. "I'm Morgan McCoy. I'm really glad to see you recovering after that scare you gave me."

Trying not to cough, she stared at him, his dark hair, his steel-blue eyes that could be as hard as iron when he was concentrating and working on a deal. Or someone had made him extremely unhappy, which she hadn't seen very often. But most of the time, those amazing eyes were extremely serious, like now. And full of concern for her—he was actually looking at her, seeing her in all her washed-out glory.

Her heart kicked up to Olympic race mode.

She wasn't used to seeing him actually noticing her. But then, she wasn't part of his inner circle in the office. Most of the time, when she saw him, it was from a distance as she was helping Mrs. Beasley. Mrs. Beasley was very protective of Morgan and who got access to him. She had even warned Amber when she was hired that there was a great divide between him and almost everyone who worked for him. Amber assumed it was to keep the hired help from trying to get their claws into the boss. Mrs. Beasley was also very protective of all those who worked in the office and Amber had no complaints against Mrs. Beasley. She had really liked her and had come to like her job. And that was why she really kept her infatuation of her boss to herself.

And she did have an infatuation.

She feared that if Mrs. Beasley had any clue that she was infatuated with him that her time on the job might be limited.

"Do I need to get the doctor? You look like you're stunned. Are you feeling okay?"

"Oh, sorry. I'm fine, thanks to you. Mr. McCoy, I can't believe you saved me."

Confusion crinkled his brow and his expression as he studied her. "Sorry for me saving you?"

"No, I'm glad you rescued me. I'm sorry I nearly drowned and you had to get wet."

His gaze sharpened. "You look familiar. Do I know you?"

He didn't recognize her. And, why should he? "I-I work for you," she stuttered.

It was his turn to look stunned. He studied her more closely. "Work for me? Here at the resort in Kauai? You looked familiar but I couldn't place you. I thought I might have seen you at the resort."

"No, not at the resort. I'm, I'm from your home office. I flew in today to help Mrs. Beasley. I'm supposed to be at work in the morning."

His brows etched deeper. "You flew in to help Mrs. Beasley?" He took that in with a thoughtfulness; she could practically see his mind working.

"I'm one of Mrs. Beasley's assistants and I've been

her main assistant on this buyout. She had me fly out to help with something that you are going to be doing." It was sure getting hot in the tiny hospital room. "I had never been to Hawaii or Kauai, so when I got here I thought I would take a swim since it was maybe the only free time I would have while here. I'm sorry. I wasn't expecting the current."

"You don't have anything to be sorry about. The currents get crazy sometimes, especially with a storm brewing offshore. And Mrs. Beasley has every right to fly someone in. I'm just confused because though you do look familiar, I can't place you in my office."

She lifted a hand to her hair, feeling vulnerable and hating the feeling. She knew she looked terrible. Her hair was in a real mess and for all she knew, she could have mascara running down her face. She hadn't had time to think, much less look in a mirror. She probably looked like a drowned rat. Her cheeks heated at the thought. On top of that, he didn't remember her at all.

But why was she upset? He barely ever glimpsed her. "There's really no reason why you would recognize me. I work in the other part of the building. This is as close to you as I've ever been. I'm Mrs. Beasley's assistant, not your assistant. There's a lot of people who work for you." She was rambling, an old habit she had believed she'd overcome. Apparently not.

She suddenly felt very weary.

He crossed his arms, his shoulders tensed, stretching the polo shirt as he searched her face. "How long have you worked for me?"

He was very persistent, but she already knew that about him.

"About a year."

He raked a hand through his thick, dark hair, looking clearly disturbed. "That's too long for me not to recognize you. Anyway, you're okay—that's all that matters so far. I'm stunned that I wouldn't know someone from my own office after a year but that's not what we're going to worry about right now. We're going to worry about whether you're okay. Has the doctor been in to see you?"

"No. The nurse went to get him. I'm afraid I might be late for work in the morning. I don't think they're going to release me until the morning. She said something about overnight."

"Don't worry about that. I'll call Mrs. Beasley in just a few minutes. And I'll make arrangements to have you picked up in the morning after we hear what the doctor has to say."

She really was out of it. She felt so confused. No one would ever believe she had a degree and a very impressive resume. "Thank you for your concern but I'm fine. I can find my own way back to the hotel. There's really no need for you to go to all this trouble." She'd been used to being on her own most of her life, so getting a taxi was nothing.

His brows dipped and those concerned blue eyes shot a little irritation. "No, there's a good reason. You work for me—we're going to take care of you. The car will come for you and Mrs. Beasley will too. So, anything you need, you ask for it." And then he turned and walked out the door.

Amber stared after him. This was the weirdest day of her life. She'd flown across the ocean, then nearly drowned in the ocean, and her boss had rescued her. Her boss, who hadn't even known she worked for him. Or that she had a terrible case of unrequited love for him.

It was really, really ridiculous and she wasn't at all sure how she had let herself get to this point.

CHAPTER TWO

Morgan called Mrs. Beasley the moment he was on the road, driving back toward Poipu.

She answered on the first ring. "Hello, Mr. McCoy." Her voice was smooth and efficient as always. Mrs. Beasley had been with him for years and was his most trusted employee and friend, and yet he could not get her to call him Morgan.

"Mrs. B, can you tell me what there is to know about the woman who flew in this morning? Her name is Amber Rhodes and she said she was supposed to be helping you this week?"

"You've already met Amber?"

"Yes, I have. I had to pull her out of the Pacific earlier. She almost drowned outside the resort."

"What?" she gasped. "I knew we had an emergency but I didn't hear anything else. Please tell me she is okay."

"She is but we didn't know who she was." He told her what had happened, giving her the short version. He was still reeling from the whole occurrence. "I didn't know we were expecting her. Is everything all right?"

"I'm so glad she is all right. Poor dear. And I was going to tell you but this happened before I informed you. To be honest, Mr. McCoy, I haven't been feeling well and I was worried that with all the help you were going to need on this deal that I better call in a backup since I was worried I might not be up for the job. I didn't really start feeling bad until we were on the plane. Rest assured, Amber is excellent. She's been with us for thirteen and a half months, just over a year, and she's been helping on the deal all month. I felt confident she could step in and take up my position for this. But now, I'm so sorry that she's in the hospital or that she nearly drowned. I can't believe it."

"She's fine. I spoke with her and she expects to be released in the morning. I told her that we would arrange to have her picked up. But I'll take care of that—you take care of yourself. Can I get you anything? If you're not feeling well, then, by all means, you take off. I don't know if you know this, Mrs. B, but I've gotten used to you being around. I can't ever imagine a time when you weren't doing your job. Is everything okay? Is this a virus or cold or something more serious?"

"Nothing terribly bad. I've been feeling very tired lately. I just have moments when I'm exhausted, so I've been seeing a doctor. I'm having some autoimmune issues that I'm now taking some supplements to help."

Morgan was immediately worried about his personal assistant. Over the years, she had become much more to him than just an assistant. Even though he didn't always show it, he was very fond of her. He could trust her with anything. She even knew about the requirements of his grandfather's will and he had told no one else. She, however, knew everything.

"If you need to go ahead and fly back home, I'll have the jet take you. I can push this deal back a few weeks. With all that I have going on, you know what

I'm talking about with the will, I might take a few days off myself."

"You—take off? Now I know you're just saying that to make me feel better. You, Morgan McCoy, don't ever take off, though it would be good for you. This thing with your grandfather has you stressed—though you would never admit it. That's another reason why I didn't want you to worry about me. My job is to worry about you."

"Mrs. B, I don't know if you realize this but I'm a grown man and have been for a very long time. I can take care of myself. And yes, you're absolutely right—I'm really conflicted about what my grandfather has done. But I'll get through this. We're worrying about you right now. Take the rest of the day off. I'll be in the office in about thirty minutes and I don't want to find you there. I want you to go up to your suite and relax. Call room service, go to the spa on the company, and just enjoy the rest of the time here if you don't want to go back home."

"Thank you. That sounds lovely, but I need to check on Amber."

"I'll take care of her."

"I'll tell you what, I'll relax but I'll be in my suite to help her, and to meet with her if she's up to working after her ordeal."

"That sounds fine, as long as you rest. I'll let you know tomorrow about her. If you need to meet with Ms. Rhodes, then you call her to your suite and work from there while you have your feet up and resting. If I need anything from you, I'll call you."

"That actually sounds like a very nice idea. And I can work like that with Amber. She can be our go-between if I don't want to use the telephone." She chuckled.

"You do it however you want to do it. But whatever you do, go to your room now. That's an order, young lady." He laughed when she laughed. He had really been blessed when he had hired her right after he'd taken over running the company. She had a resume that was out of this world and she was the best assistant he could have. And if she thought this Amber Rhodes could fill in for her, then he could trust that.

If she felt like it after nearly drowning.

It still bothered him that he hadn't recognized her. She was pretty; he assumed she was very efficient or she wouldn't be working for Mrs. B. So he already knew that she had to be a go-getter or she wouldn't be his employee. But was he that much removed from the people who worked in the home office with him that he couldn't even recognize their faces? Then again, Ms. Rhodes had been pale, her hair had been slicked down, and he had a feeling that she probably didn't look exactly like she normally would. Still, it bothered him.

He pulled into his private parking at the resort and got out, jogged up the stairs to his private entrance, and took the elevator to the top floor. This wasn't just his entrance but when they had high-profile guests, it was another way for them to be able to come and go without being seen or followed. His cousin Denton used it when he stayed at the resort. Now that he had a couple of hit country albums, he was sometimes stalked by the paparazzi, so he appreciated the secured entrance.

Once Morgan got to his room, he yanked off his clothes and jumped into the shower. The hot water helped him relax a bit and he felt better. He dressed quickly then headed down the main elevator to his office. Mrs. Beasley was not there, so he called his limo service and put them on call for tomorrow to go to the hospital to pick up Ms. Rhodes whenever the doctor released her.

He pulled up his computer and for the first time ever, he just stared at the screen. His thoughts were consumed with what his grandfather had done and that he could lose this business. His lawyers had assured him that there was no way to get out of it and that meant he had to find a wife. But he wasn't yet willing to give up and told them to keep looking.

He wanted to hold onto his resorts. He was thirty-five years old and despite being the age of settling down, he'd failed miserably at it once... After that, he had no plans to ever do it again. Gold diggers in this business were sometimes too close for comfort. Because of that, he had strategically put teams in place to shield him from any kind of controversy and people who might have ulterior motives for meeting him.

Obviously, Mrs. B and the others had done a good job of keeping people at bay considering he didn't even notice people who worked for him for a year.

McCoy Stonewall Resorts and Hotels Division part

of McCoy Enterprises was a large company, but to not even recognize a woman who worked closely to his personal assistant meant either he was too far removed from his people or he had become too far removed on purpose and wasn't paying attention to the things around him that mattered. People mattered; his business mattered; his business was built on people. But maybe he had become so occupied with his work that he stopped looking around at anything else that mattered.

He could tell that when Amber Rhodes had realized that he didn't recognize her, it had been a little bit of an insult to her. She'd covered it up quickly but he saw it in her eyes. He'd also noticed that she'd been very professional despite what she had been through and he couldn't help being intrigued by a woman with that much composure or discipline.

* * *

Amber was shocked when someone from the resort arrived the next morning with a bag that had some of her clothing in it, her makeup, and toiletries. The lady handed her a phone; Mrs. Beasley was on the other end of the line.

"Amber, dear, I'm terribly sorry for what happened to you yesterday. I'm so very glad you're okay but tell me about how you are today."

And so the conversation went. She had sent the things over so that Amber would have something fresh to wear. When she learned that she was feeling perfectly fine and ready to work, Mrs. Beasley sounded relieved and informed Amber that Mr. McCoy was sending a limo for her when she was released. Amber didn't argue; she did, after all, work for a billionaire and there were perks like limousine rides that came with the territory.

Now dressed, her hair pulled back in the slick fashion that she normally wore it in for work, coiled into a tight bun at the nape of her neck, Amber felt more like herself. She wore a pair of charcoal slacks with a pair of closed-toed black pumps that she always included for her work and a cream-toned, satiny blouse, and no jewelry. She believed in being nondescript when she worked because she was supposed to be a behind-the-scenes assistant and she didn't like to draw attention to herself.

After the doctor came and released her, they wheeled her downstairs to the front entrance to wait for the car that was picking her up. No sooner than she was wheeled outside than a slick black Mercedes pulled from the curb and stopped in front of her. Her stomach felt queasy when she saw none other than Morgan McCoy step from the low-slung, luxury sports car.

Dear goodness, the man took her breath away. He wore a white oxford with dark slacks and boots. The man was a Texan, after all. A very high-powered Texas businessman who liked his black boots. And she enjoyed seeing him in those boots. She liked knowing that he had come from ranching roots. She always wondered whether he wore them as a reminder of his roots. She came from ranching stock, though it was a very long time ago. She owned a pair as a reminder, though she didn't carry them around with her nor did she wear them often. But she had them, and cherished them because of what they reminded her of.

They wouldn't exactly go with her slacks nor with her pencil skirts when she wore them, but she did love them. Loved when she'd been a kid and had a horse…and a family and a very small ranch. Her heart ached for all of those memories…all that was before that moment in time that had stolen her real life away from her, leaving only the memories.

Memories that were so long ago, they felt like dreams instead of the reality she'd truly once lived.

Morgan rounded the end of the car and her heart raced as he strode toward her. He smiled and her knees melted. "You look a little different than you did yesterday. I'm assuming Mrs. B sent over some clothes for you."

His gaze swept over her and a buzz of awareness vibrated through her. She needed to be very careful. She took a short, calming breath, trying to quiet the irrational feelings. "She did. Mrs. Beasley is very efficient. She also told me that she wasn't feeling well and that I would be taking over her duties while here. I thought it was very curious when she had me fly in. She's never sick—well, she's had a few days when she's seemed to be more tired than usual. But she's a powerhouse. She has me a little worried."

"I appreciate your concern for her. I feel the same

way but she assured me she would be fine and there is nothing to be alarmed about. I have her relaxing and taking advantage of her suite and room service. We'll do a little pampering for her while she's here and I'll let you help me with any letters or paperwork that I need to have done. We will have to make a trip up to Princeville to look at the property. But right now, how are you feeling today?"

He reached for the small overnight bag she was holding that her things had been brought over in. Amber didn't let go of the handle in time and his hand closed over hers. Instantly, her stomach felt bottomless and butterflies spread through her, making her feel fluttery and surreal. It was not an uncommon thing for the butterflies to appear any time she saw her boss. His touch was a completely new sensation. Her eyes flew to his. He was watching her. *Did she see attraction in his eyes? No, surely not.*

"I'll take this bag." He tugged and she let go. He opened the car door for her and she sank into the plush interior.

She had expected a limo with a driver, not him and his Mercedes. It was very odd for him to have picked her up, but then, he had rescued her. *Did he feel responsible for her?* She was the one who felt obliged and grateful to him.

When he had stored the case in the trunk, he slid into the seat beside her. She was struck by the intimacy of the car interior when he closed the door and turned to her.

"Do you need anything before we head back to Poipu and the resort?"

"N-no, I'm fine. And I need to say again that I'm very grateful to you for rescuing me."

He shrugged, his attention focused like a laser on her. "I'm just glad I was there. Thankful you are sitting here with me now."

"I am too. But you really didn't have to come pick me up yourself. I know you have much more important things to be doing."

His brows creased and his blue gaze sharpened. "Nothing is more important than you at this moment." His voice deepened with conviction.

She didn't know what to say to that, so she just nodded and placed a hand on her stomach to steady the butterflies that now threatened to have her babbling like a schoolgirl in love any moment. Accepting her nod as assurance, he put the car into drive and eased out of the hospital's covered portico. She stared at the road, feeling as if she'd gone for a swim yesterday and entered a time warp or something.

The strong current had swept her away into now very dangerous territory.

CHAPTER THREE

Morgan had not planned to pick Amber up that morning but the more he thought about it, the more he couldn't just let a car go pick her up after what she had been through. Now he looked at her in the passenger seat and realized she looked as if she felt very uncomfortable with him.

He almost hadn't recognized her when he'd pulled up, and it gave him insight into why he might not have recognized her from work...she'd pulled her hair back in an extremely severe bun. There wasn't a hair out of place and he could swear the skin at her temples was straining from the tension. It was slicked back so tight and twisted into the thick, taut bun at the nape of her neck. He tried not to stare and had to fight the strong urge to pull the pins out and let her hair fall about her shoulders again.

How had she done that? She had a little bit of color to her skin today and had a cool air of sophistication about her. Yesterday, she had been pale and vulnerable-looking but there had been a softness to her that he didn't see this morning. She was pretty but she was all business.

He put the car in drive and took them out of the hospital parking lot and turned back onto the main road.

"You're feeling better today? No side effects?" Small talk wasn't his best skill. He glanced at her and met her gaze as she glanced from the road to him. His pulse quickened, startling him. He yanked his head back around to focus on the road. *What was this?*

"I am." She sounded a little breathless, making his pulse race more.

What? His fingers tightened on the wheel. He searched for something else to say. But the only thing he wanted to ask her was why she was wearing her hair like that. And that was not what he should be asking an employee. *And why did he want to know, anyway?*

"I was ready to go home last night," she added. "Honestly, I was overwhelmed by how naïve I had been. Sir, I'm not one to do rash things and me going out in that water was rash. I've never been to Hawaii and had no idea about the currents. I shouldn't have gone farther than wading. But no, the water felt so good and I just felt a little out of character and ventured into the water. And then I was swimming and the water got deep very quickly. One minute, I was close to shore and then I was towed out and struggling." Her voice shook slightly.

The sound had sympathy shooting through him and he wanted to comfort her.

"You missed the signs, and you were too far down the beach—the undercurrent is very bad down there closer to the cliffs. That's why there weren't a lot of people in the water. The storm made it dangerous. You just didn't realize."

He looked back at her and saw that her eyes were closed. He studied her briefly. She didn't seem to be a person who was used to making mistakes. If he was right about that, they had that in common because he wasn't used to making mistakes either, so he could understand her frustration. Maybe even her embarrassment. "There are a lot of beautiful beaches here but you have to be careful. Always watch for the signs. The resort has some really nice swimming pools if you don't want to get back into the ocean after what happened. It would be understandable."

He would be more comfortable if she would stay in the pool because he didn't want her drowning while she was here on his watch. And he wasn't sure how well she could swim. Better safe than sorry.

"Oh, don't worry—I won't be going back into the water. As of this morning, I'm on your time and I will not be taking any more time off for leisure like that."

The lush greenery of the landscape passed in a blur as he processed her words. "You'll have time off. I'm not a taskmaster. I would just rather you swam in the pool."

"But Mrs. B said I'll be on call the entire time I'm here. This deal is too important. I assumed that meant we needed to work some long hours like you normally do."

He rubbed his forehead. He had had this business trip planned and had come as planned but his heart wasn't in it. What his granddaddy was forcing him to do had him distracted and he'd barely been thinking about the Princeville deal. "Yes, you're right, the resort in Princeville is why we're here. I had planned to go there this afternoon but that was before your situation happened. We'll put it off."

"No, please don't do that because of me. I'm ready to help you. I can do my job." There was almost panic in her voice.

"It's okay. Don't worry—we can do it later."

"Mr. McCoy, I came here to work and that is what I intend to do." She had a determined grit in her tone.

"If you're certain. But a girl shouldn't come to paradise and not have free time to enjoy it. You'll do that before you leave. I'll be going there later this afternoon and will require you to go with me if you are up to it."

"I'm ready."

"We'll be staying overnight, so prepare a bag. You'll have your own room, of course."

"Of course. Mrs. Beasley told me to be prepared to travel to the resort with you."

"She did?" He thought that was strange but then,

she must have anticipated she would feel too bad to travel.

"Yes, I assume so. But, don't worry, I've traveled a few times for her to gather information needed on certain resorts, so I know a little about the process. I reported directly to Mrs. Beasley."

"I see. I knew that she got information for me on certain things sometimes but I hadn't realized you were one of the people she used to gather information on resorts." How could he when he hadn't even known she existed? "So what kind of information did you gather?"

"Usually just for an overnight trip to check out resort procedures. I made sure that the managers were doing their job well...without them realizing they were being checked on."

He laughed. "You were our spy. You went incognito."

She blushed. "Yes. I didn't really know how to say that, but yes. That's what I do sometimes. I'm never there for very long and no one knows who I am. I let her know if managers are doing what they are supposed to be doing when there are problems at certain resorts."

"Now that I know what you normally do, I understand why I don't always see you. Because I actually do recognize you now with your hair pulled back."

He watched her hand flutter to her hair and she ran a hand lightly over the severe style. She looked almost self-conscious. He hadn't meant to make her uncomfortable.

"I wear my hair so that it's very business-like. I like to keep a very professional appearance."

He almost laughed. But he didn't because he realized she was being completely serious. "You do it well."

The urge to tell her she could let her hair down and loosen up a little bit was strong but he resisted. He could see why she would be chosen by Mrs. B to fly to the various resorts because she could check in and not be very memorable with her appearance as it was. But his thoughts went back to the woman he had seen sitting in the hospital bed yesterday. She'd been vulnerable-looking with her hair down and her slight color to her cheeks. And though she had not been at her best because of what she'd been through, she was very memorable.

He kept his thoughts to himself, not wanting to cross any lines between boss and employee. But he definitely liked her hair better down.

He stared at the road and concentrated on the red light coming up. There was a chicken walking across the street and he didn't want to hit one of the Kauai chickens. The golden-brown bird with the red feather topper and dark wings took its time as it strutted across in front of the stopped vehicles. When it made it safely to the other side, the red light seemed to know it and turned green. He drove safely forward through it.

"That chicken was amazing. It was almost like the red light knew the chicken was crossing the road."

He laughed. "You sound like you're going to tell me jokes now. How did the chicken cross the road?"

She laughed. "Very slowly."

They both laughed. He met her gaze and her eyes were actually twinkling. *She had beautiful eyes when they lit up like that.* He focused on the road.

"There's another chicken! Oh my goodness. I had heard there were chickens on the islands but I didn't know they just walked along the side of the road like that."

"They're here and if you were to drive up the Waimea Canyon, they are at the top of the mountains there too."

"Really? So they're everywhere?"

"Yes. Maybe in your free time you need to take a drive up. It's not that far of a drive to the southern end of the island from the resort since we're in Poipu. In your free time, before we fly out, that would be a nice trip for you. Did you book a flight home?"

"No. I actually didn't book my flight here. Like I told you, Mrs. Beasley made all the arrangements. My ticket arrived by courier and she said she will book it when it's time for me to leave."

"You're welcome to fly with us back on the private jet."

"Oh, but you don't usually fly with anyone other than your assistant."

"You are my assistant for this trip."

"Yes, that's right." She clasped her hands tightly in her lap and looked flustered.

He wasn't sure why but for some reason he was

letting his guard down with her, just a little. But still, for him, that was unusual.

They made the drive back to the resort and he told her a little bit about the resort that they were going to look at. She took notes and when they arrived, he pulled in under the portico and told her to meet him back downstairs after lunch. He watched her walk through the doors and disappear. His pulse raced a little bit, watching her leave. She was very feminine and he couldn't help it; he wanted to see her hair down again.

What is wrong with you, McCoy? He turned to the waiting bellhop, an older man who had worked for them for several years. "Sid, here's the keys. But we'll be using the car again in an hour. You doing okay today?"

"I'm doing great. My family is, too, and thank you for the tickets for the sunset cruise. My wife really enjoyed it. It's funny that you can live in paradise but the everyday grind still creeps in and we don't do the special things. I appreciate you giving me a wakeup call not to take this all for granted, or my beautiful wife."

Morgan smiled. "I was just trying to do something nice for you. It's not every day you celebrate your fortieth wedding anniversary. And I wouldn't want you taking Mallie for granted either. She's a keeper."

"And I plan to keep her for another eighty." He grinned wide. "I'm still waiting to see you find a beautiful wife. The little lady who just left looks very sweet."

"She is very nice." It was true, she was nice, and he didn't bother pointing out to the older man that she was his assistant and it was a strictly business relationship. Instead, he headed to his suite, deep in thought.

He had a computer call set up with his brothers and had just enough time to get to his office for the call. He had decisions to make. The clock was ticking.

CHAPTER FOUR

"Why are y'all grinning like that?" Morgan stared at Wade and Todd on the computer screen. This was their monthly board meeting and their time to find out whether he was going to fight for his resorts. Which meant find a wife and give in to his granddaddy's demands.

Todd laughed, deep and with complete delight at Morgan's dilemma. "You know why we're grinning. We're wondering how you're going to handle this little kink Granddaddy has thrown at you."

Todd had hated the idea as much as Morgan did, at least until he met Ginny and fell head over heels off the cliff of love. Morgan held his tongue, refusing to take his brother's bait. *Let him gloat.*

"Knock it off, Todd. Give him a break," Wade said. "We know that your mind is churning and that the control part of you is having a fit. I feel bad for you but we've all had to deal with this."

"Yup." Todd laughed. "I bet you haven't slept a wink since knowing it was your turn."

Morgan rubbed his temple and sighed. His patience was gone. "Okay, you're right, Todd. I have been uptight. But lay off. I told you both from the very beginning at the reading of Granddaddy's will, when we learned what was in store for Wade, that I was not happy about this. And nothing has changed."

"We know that." Concern took the place of Wade's laughter. "But you're going to have to do it or you're going to lose McCoy Stonewall Hotel and Resort Division. Morgan, you know very well you can't do that. You have built that leg of the company into what it is. You're going to have to hop on this runaway train that is Granddaddy's last wishes and find a wife."

"Wade's right," Todd agreed. "The clock is ticking. It's been a week since we met in Cal's office and learned your specifications for holding onto the resorts. Have you put any thought into it? Have you started looking for your Mrs. McCoy?"

Morgan's jaw tightened and every muscle in his body followed. "I came here to think about it, but I'm not rushing into anything. I've still got my lawyers trying to find a loophole."

Wade looked as if he couldn't believe he was still resisting the inevitable. "You know they're not going to find a loophole. Granddaddy left no loopholes. We all know that. Look, you can do this. You know contracts better than any of us. Just find someone who isn't going to drive you crazy for three months, preferably someone you enjoy being around. You never know what will happen. What would Granddad think if all three of us actually found love because of his crazy idea?"

"Happily-ever-after because of Granddaddy forcing me to do something against my will is not happening. I won't let it. If I do this, it will be with a really strong prenuptial agreement and it will clearly state that no matter what, it is over in three months. There will not be any falling in love for me. I'm glad for you guys—I really am. I mean, it's hard to believe you have an ultimatum like this and both of you come out in love. And looking to have kids. But Granddaddy will not take control of my life like this."

Todd shook his head, resignation in his eyes. "Morgan, it's been amazing. I was as much a critic of the whole thing as you are but—I never expected to fall in love. And miraculously, it happened, so don't go into this with a closed mind. If it could happen to me and Wade, it could happen to you. And I know you don't want to talk about it, but we all know Shannon hurt you. I know that whole sad story, but move forward and be open to this."

"Todd's right," Wade agreed, sympathy etching his features. "It's time to move on."

Exasperated, his finger hovered over the disconnect button. He wanted to end the call. But that wouldn't be right. Instead, he gritted through tight lips, "It won't happen. If I do it, it's just a business decision. I'll make a proposition and if whoever I make it to doesn't want it, I'll find someone else who I believe has something to gain from a business deal. It will only be a straightforward proposition. That's it."

Both of his brothers shook their heads at his close-minded approach. He understood they were happy so they couldn't fathom that he wasn't going to have anybody telling him who and when to get married and that he wasn't taking kindly to it.

When and if he married again for real, it would be his—and only his—decision. It would be completely calculated and every aspect of his bride's life would be sifted through before he went through with the marriage. And there certainly wouldn't be any money tied up in it other than an agreed upon prenup. No one would ever pull the wool over his eyes again.

He'd been down that road with Shannon, by his own stupidity when he'd married a gold-digger and he'd had to live with the consequences. He despised thinking about it even now, his stomach turning. He'd realized early into the marriage that his wife had lied about her feelings toward him and had no interest in anything but his money. He'd tried to hang on, find a way to make it work, but knowing his wife was living it up with other men when he was away had made that plan fall apart. But then, while his lawyers got his divorce documents ready she learned she had a genetic disease that was incurable and fast-acting. It had been tragic and complicated everything.

He hadn't been able to go through with the divorce and had continued the farce of a marriage until her death six months later. It had been sad, ridiculous and tragic. And he should have never let himself fall for her deception in the first place.

And he wouldn't ever let it happen again.

So if he chose to do this deal of his granddaddy's it would be strictly business.

Amber had been excited as she'd brought her overnight bag downstairs. Her insides were jittery as she saw him waiting for her beside his car.

"Hi." She heard the breathy tone and hoped he didn't realize how excited she was to be spending time alone with him. "I hope I didn't keep you waiting?"

"Not at all. Let me take that." He took her bag; their fingers grazed and sent her pulse racing at that smallest touch. She tried to gather her composure as he stowed the bag in the trunk.

She hurried around to her side of the car, climbed in

and waited for him. She took a couple of huge, deep breaths. *Get a hold of yourself, girlfriend.*

He slid in behind the wheel. "Buckled up? Here we go."

Moments later, her excitement congealed in the pit of her stomach as Morgan drove the Mercedes up to a helicopter pad.

"What?" she gasped and swiveled toward him. "We're going in a helicopter?"

"You have a problem with that?"

She blinked rapid-fire and the helicopter did not disappear. Her stomach churned and she felt nauseous; her mouth was bitterly dry. Surely, she wouldn't throw up.

"S-sure I'm ready." She tried to hide her fear with a big smile. A smile she wasn't really feeling. She had never been in a helicopter. Hanging in the air by four blades wasn't her idea of fun. It ranked right there with jumping out of an airplane with a little tiny parachute. And neither things were on her bucket list. She liked her feet planted firmly on the ground. Getting into a large aircraft or even a private jet was not the easiest thing for her to do but it was at least a proven form of transportation.

He got out of the car. She licked her lips then planted them together firmly as she got out of the car. *Relax, you can do this.* The loudness of the helicopter motor and the wind from the rotating blades hit her at the same time. Dear Lord, she wanted to run.

Halt. Stand your ground; this is your job—and do not throw up.

Morgan McCoy probably didn't have a fondness for people getting sick in helicopter rides with him, or running away from them either. It wasn't professional and she was always professional. Well, maybe not when she was drowning but all other times, she was and proud of it.

Swallowing hard, she willed the metallic taste in her mouth to go away. *Seriously, go away.* Morgan grabbed their bags from the trunk of the beautiful, black luxury car and she wished with everything in her that she was still inside, cruising down the road toward Princeville.

But she wasn't.

Morgan strode purposefully toward the chopper and she just stood there, watching the blades rotating as the wind from it blew strands of her hair from her tight bun and blew her skirt up. She slapped her hands to her skirt and secured it to her thighs. *Of all days for her to choose to wear business attire with a little less severe cut.* The skirt had just a little bit of a flounce to it, just enough to threaten a little more of her leg than she normally showed. Now it threatened to show more of her backside, if she weren't careful.

She would be embarrassed if her skirt got away from her in front of her boss. It was mortifying enough to know he'd fished her out of the ocean yesterday. Thankfully, she'd had her one-piece swimsuit on and not the bikini she'd been tempted to bring along on the Hawaii trip.

She was rather modest but had almost let herself get something a little more tropical-feeling than the black conservative one-piece she wore for this trip. Even if she had only been planning to swim for one afternoon.

Morgan turned; their gazes connected and she knew she had to make a move. She took a deep breath and forced herself to cross to him, ducking slightly as she hurried beneath the churning blades. They weren't churning any more than her stomach.

When she reached him, Morgan stopped her with a hand on her arm. "Wait," he shouted over the roar of the helicopter. He studied her. "Are you okay? You look pale. Are you not comfortable riding in this helicopter?"

The man had a way of reading people. "I'm fine," she practically yelled.

"I don't think so." He leaned close to her ear, his breath tickling her ear enticingly.

He was so close and she turned to answer him. Their faces were close and she felt breathless...and momentarily forgot about her churning stomach. "Okay, it will be my first time to ride on a helicopter. What's not fun about that?"

His lips twitched, something she found very intriguing. As he leaned closer to her ear, the wind from the blades surrounded them. His arm went around her shoulders in a protective action. "I can promise you that these guys who fly this helicopter know what they're doing. And if you'll relax, I'll have them show you a little bit of the island from the air that you won't see any other way. Kauai is an amazing place. That's why they use it in so many movies."

She was very aware because she had looked it up before her trip—Kauai was the home of many a movie, such as *Seven Nights and Seven Days* or something like that starring Harrison Ford, whom she had a crush on growing up, and *Mighty Joe Young*, which she had also enjoyed growing up. Watching a gorilla running across the land was a pretty cool sight. And of course, *Jurassic Park*—if she remembered it right, helicopters didn't always make it out during the movie. Not the memories she needed to be paying attention to at the moment.

"Great. That would be very nice." She plastered on a smile that was as fake as the enthusiasm of her words.

"Okay, we better get on then." He helped her step into the chopper.

She took the seat and immediately grabbed the seat belt. She was in a daze as she was handed a headset and Morgan helped her put it on. Blissfully, the noise diminished.

Her nerves did not and moments later, the piece of metal and motor lifted from the ground. She clamped her eyes closed and fought down the need to scream as she grabbed Morgan's hand and held on for dear life.

* * *

"Amber. You need to open your eyes now," Morgan urged over the headset a short while later.

Amber had only peeked a few times during the ride to the waterfall and now she opened her eyes very slowly and forced herself to look at it. Her breath caught at the up-close sight of massive water falling outside the helicopter's windows. It was close. The chopper was slowly lowering down, down, down, beside the falling water toward the pool that she glanced at. Then she leaned closer to Morgan, his rich cologne drawing her closer. She was still gripping his hand. She knew she needed to let go but she couldn't bring herself to do it. She had dreamed of touching him…she shouldn't have but she had—and this was not helping her get over her feelings for him.

When she had come to work at McCoy Stonewall Enterprises, she had no idea she would get this infatuation. Yes, she had done her due diligence and she had known who he was, but she was not one prone to getting crushes on people. But the first time she had been in close proximity to him and he had met her gaze with those amazing steel-blue eyes of his, it had locked her into the completely unhealthy problem that she had. And he had been unfazed, because he hadn't even recognized that she worked for him.

But, here she was, in a helicopter beside the *Jurassic Park* waterfall, holding his hands and he was probably thinking that she was some psycho not worthy of the position she held with his company. Yes, she was probably not going to get this chance again. Still, if that was the case, she might as well enjoy touching him while she could.

She focused on the waterfall. As they continued, she saw that they were heading straight to a pool of water and what looked like an area they could land on. She looked up at Morgan. "Are we landing on that?"

He laughed. *He had such a nice laugh.* "I thought we might. Give you a chance to collect yourself. If you think you can get back on the bird."

She nodded. "I can get back on." Although she was worried that maybe if she got back on, she wouldn't get to hold his hand again. "Seeing the waterfall will be very nice."

A nice memory for her when she went home and never saw him again. Because she would probably be fired. But then again, he was being very nice. Very nice, and relaxed. She went back to the waterfall and tried to relax herself. She had never seen Morgan McCoy relaxed. One more reason for her to be infatuated with him. She was really in deep.

But she realized thinking about Morgan helped her not to think about that she was in a small piece of metal being held up in the air by four very fast-moving blades that could at any moment hit a flock of birds and maybe crash them into the waterfall. She closed her eyes and forced herself again to think about Morgan instead and how nice his hand felt holding hers. Yes, that calmed her.

The small piece of metal landed and the engine and blades blissfully shut down. And at last she relaxed. But she didn't let go of Morgan's hand; although he had released hers, she was still clinging to his.

"Okay, we can get off. Do you think you can get out on your own?" the pilot asked.

"We've got it, Hank." Morgan opened the door with

his free hand then tugged her to follow him. "Careful now," he said to her as she wobbled, stepping from the bird to the ground.

Her legs were weak. She looked back at Morgan. "Okay, I think I can give you your hand back."

He smiled. "Very well, if you're sure."

She wasn't sure but she did anyway, with much regret. "I'm sure you need to let the blood flow back into your fingers."

"Thanks." He chuckled. Standing beside her, he looked so in control. "What do you think?" He nodded toward the falls.

"This is gorgeous."

"Come on. Let's go over here." He moved toward the waterfall.

She followed and Hank remained at the helicopter.

Now that she was off the helicopter, she could actually relax. She looked up, amazed at how far down they had come in the helicopter. "That is way up there—how amazing. Honestly, in the movie, I thought that they made it seem bigger than it actually was."

"There are times it is actually smaller. Depends on how much rain they've gotten, on how much water comes over the fall. I don't really know how they filmed it or if, you know, they used portions of another waterfall. I know it is beautiful. It's something neat to experience. I hope you're glad I forced you to come down."

"I am. I'm not sure I'll ever get over it." She laughed and felt the relief of it. She wasn't sure she'd ever get back on a helicopter, but her job required her to get back on this one. "I'm not sure I'll ever be back to this waterfall, so I'm really glad that you detoured and brought me here."

He grinned; she was fairly sure he knew she was about to say *never get back on a helicopter*. But, thankfully, he didn't say anything. "To be honest, I've been here once. I don't normally go sightseeing when I'm on the island. I'm usually here for business and a majority of the time I stay in the resort. I walk out on to the lava rocks and look down at the sea turtles. That's where I was when I saw you in the water. Other than that, I'm not usually out looking like this. It's nice. Reminds me why we have a resort here."

"You do seem to work all the time, if you don't mind me saying so."

The look that crossed his face said he agreed, but he didn't say so. Instead, he turned his head to look up at the waterfall. She continued to study his sculpted profile. A man like him was driven. A man like him would never make a family man in her mind, despite knowing he'd been married before. She had career dreams, she had dreams of family too. *So why*, she asked herself, *did she have an infatuation with the man who was definitely not marriage material in her mind?*

"Do you ever think you're going to slow down?" The question came out before she could get her brain working again. She would just say it was the ride in the helicopter that had her asking questions, digging into his personal life.

He met her gaze. "I don't know. My brothers have recently settled down, although they were much more settled down before marrying than I was or am. I travel a lot, as you know, and I really love what I do…and it didn't work out in my previous marriage. So, I don't know—good question. But I have a situation right now that has me a little off my normal game."

"Really? I didn't know that happened."

He kind of gave her a grimace. "Whew, you are

59

fairly direct."

"I'm sorry. I'm probably overstepping my position. But, well, I figure why not. I have been observing you for the time I've been at the company and I have never seen you off your game. I wouldn't have guessed you were now. Well, you detoured to this waterfall for me and you rescued me from the ocean. So maybe that is a little abnormal from a daily routine. But if you're off your game, you're hiding it very well."

He crossed his arms and studied her. His gaze searched deep; those steel-blue eyes of his seemed to look all the way into her soul. She didn't need anybody looking at her soul. She shifted from foot to foot. "Why are you looking at me like that?"

"What do you want? Out of life? Do you have any needs, a dream that you have that you're trying to fulfill? Do you have a financial need that needs to be met?"

It was her turn to step back. *What?* She stared at him, completely unsure of where he was going with this very odd conversation. "And you're asking because why?"

He raked a hand through his hair, looking out of his

element suddenly. "Because I…" His lips flattened and his jaw tightened, as if he did not want to say what he was about to say. "Because the truth is, Amber, I need to find someone who is willing to take a financial trade." He halted. His gaze shifted to the waterfall, his shoulders dropping.

Amber's insides tightened with apprehension—surely, he wasn't about to proposition her and destroy everything she'd believed good about him.

"I need to contract someone for a specific purpose and I am at a loss about where to start. I have never found myself at a loss before."

Okay, this was really weird but she refused to believe bad about him. "And this proposition, I mean *contract* that you're needing, why would you need to ask me those questions? I'm your personal assistant. Are you wanting me to help you find this person?"

He looked grim. "Normally, yes. If we were looking for information on a resort we were wanting to buy or a piece of land we were wanting to buy or a problem at a resort, I would be using you for that. This is personal. My granddaddy made sure of that."

His words were low and the sound of the waterfall

landing in the pool almost caused her to miss that his grandfather was the reason for this conversation. She stepped closer to him, very curious now. "And your grandfather, why does he need you to do whatever it is he's asked you to do? Didn't your grandfather pass away? I'm fairly sure, yes, that is correct. Almost five, maybe seven months ago."

"Yes, he did. And my grandfather—you never met him; he was out of the resort business by the time you came along—turned it completely over to me. We were very much alike. Two strong-willed McCoy men don't always get along. But he had wishes before he died and he left them in his will. And he left each of his grandsons specific trials to go through to retain specific things. Both of my brothers have successfully maneuvered their requirements. Now it's my turn. My grandfather saved me for last because he knew it was going to be hardest on me."

Boy, now she was really curious and no longer worried that he was about to proposition her—*thank goodness*. Then again, the idea of this man being attracted to her would please her...it was so confusing to her. Then she remembered he'd asked about her financial situation and her confusion rushed back. "I'm still very uncertain why you need to know my financial situation or what my hopes and dreams are. Can you enlighten me on that? This is very odd."

He gave a gruff laugh. "Yes, I think you have hit the nail on the head—it is extremely odd. I think we should get back on the helicopter and head to Princeville. I need to think about this. I'll probably regret that I ever mentioned it to you, so for right now let's pretend I never said anything."

With that, he strode toward the helicopter.

She remained rooted to the grassy spot beside the water. It was very odd. Very, very odd. But she knew that Morgan McCoy had no reputation at all for soliciting women. For a moment there, she had almost thought…but no, she was mistaken. If he were looking for something like that, it wouldn't be her. *Nope.*

Feeling more curious than ever, she followed him back to the helicopter, where he was waiting with the door open. Thank goodness, the pilot hadn't started the blades yet. Morgan climbed inside then held his hand out to her. She slipped her hand into his and tried very hard to ignore the tingles of sheer delight dancing up her arm and through her chest as she climbed in behind him.

She buckled in; she didn't even blink twice. Her thoughts were on the odd contractual proposition his grandfather was requiring of him. *Yes, it was very odd.* She put her headgear on and glanced at him. He was back to being all business.

"Are you okay? Do you need my hand again or are you going to be able to do the ride from here to Princeville?"

She was embarrassed by how she'd clung to him. "I believe I can." She wasn't sure about that at all but she would act professional if it was the last thing she did. She clasped her hands together, determined to get through this without the need of her boss's hands.

CHAPTER FIVE

Morgan wasn't sure whether he had lost his mind or whether he was brilliant but in a matter of moments, he had decided that he was going to ask Amber to be his wife.

His wife for three short, very well paid months.

He just had to find out what she was motivated by. Wade had gotten Allie because she had needed some money. There was nothing wrong with that; sometimes there were situations where people needed a way out. Same thing with Todd; he had gotten Ginny to marry him because she hadn't so much needed the money but she had needed to save her vineyard. If they could do it, he could do it. He had realized that in his entire life, nothing had ever scared him when it came to business. So why was he letting this situation that his grandfather had created turn him into a...what? A sellout? He hadn't quite figured out what was wrong but the one thing he knew was he had questioned himself about this, and Morgan was not used to questioning himself. Like his grandfather had always gone with his famous gut that was great with hunches that turned out well, Morgan was the same. He made decisions, sometimes instantly and all on a gut feeling. He didn't need a lot of information; he used his gut almost as much as he used information. And when he used information, he always used his gut too.

And his gut was telling him that Amber was the woman who would consent to this. She'd sign the prenuptial agreement and look at the proposition as a business contract when she found out what he could lose if she didn't marry him. She seemed very honest and upfront. She had been herself and she hadn't been afraid to ask him questions. He liked that about her. And despite her fear of the helicopter, she had forced herself onto the chopper, and her clutching his hand hadn't been a coy ploy to hold his hand but an actual need on her part. He was pretty sure most of the trip she had no idea how hard she had clung to him.

He had put her in a situation to try her and see what came out, to see what her reaction would be. What he saw was someone with true grit and job loyalty.

She was the right one.

Then why did it feel so wrong?

Not that this had anything to do with job loyalty. It had to do with something he could do for her in the long run. She had to have a dream, had to have something that motivated her. Maybe she wanted to open her own marketing company one day. He could help her make that happen. He could give her a leg up. Even if she wasn't desperate like Allie or Ginny had been, something had to motivate her to take the deal he was going to offer her.

He thought about it all the way to Princeville as she sat quietly, thoughtfully looking out at the passing scenery. The only show that she was worried or panicked was that her hands were now clasped together so tightly they were as white as snow.

But her eyes were opened and he hoped that at some

point she was able to enjoy the beauty of this amazing island from this altitude.

He found himself contemplating how beautiful she was at this altitude. At any altitude. Her pert nose. Her pink lips, that were compressed still, had a quirk at the edges, as if she were always ready to smile. He yanked his thoughts off her beauty and looked out his window, shifting his thoughts back to his problem and contemplated his next move.

He was surprised that she hadn't pushed him on the odd statements that he had said to her. Then again, he had told her that in due time he would let her know, so as a dutiful executive admin, she was doing her job.

After they landed, the trip from the landing strip to the resort was fairly brief. Different from the southern end of Kauai, the northern tip was luscious and green, wild with the rainforest at the tip separating it from the Na Pali Coast. The area they were in now was packed with golf courses and luxury hotels, bed-and-breakfasts and resorts. It was all gorgeous but he preferred the southern tip. But if he could get this resort for his offered price, having two McCoy options on this small island paradise would be a wise decision.

At the resort, they were greeted by the bellhops and hostess, who placed a beautiful purple orchid lei around Amber's neck and a lei of tiny shells around his. He enjoyed the delight of Amber as she thanked the beautiful Polynesian woman. Moments later, they entered the lobby of the stunning resort.

"Mr. McCoy," Amber said, as she walked beside him to the front desk.

He shot her a look but refrained from smiling. "Morgan. You can call me, Morgan."

She looked momentarily flustered. "I am here to work and I think I probably shouldn't let my guard down too much calling you Morgan. Especially in front of the people you'll be meeting with, I assume then, especially I'll need to address you as Mr. McCoy."

"Actually, we're not meeting with anyone. We're here…" he leaned in close to her and whispered, "incognito."

The look on her face was priceless. "What do you mean?" she asked in hushed dismay. "They don't know you're coming?"

"No. I'm assuming the people who work here won't know who I am. If the owners happen to be here, which I looked into and they're not, I might have a problem but we're here to see how things work. To look at the property and watch the people. I want to see if the people who are staying at the resort are enjoying themselves."

She breathed a deep breath and let it out slowly. She bit her lip and then he gave her time to think. She leaned closer. "Sir, why am I here?"

She smelled delicious. Like sweet vanilla ice cream. "To help me."

"I see."

"No, I don't think you do. I realized earlier that Mrs. Beasley might not have felt well but she also has been grooming you to do this. You've been going to resorts for her and you've been our eyes and ears for a while now. I didn't know this. And I think that she probably set this up so you could be the one to help me. So that is why you're here."

"She has prepared me. She's had me look at everything on the trips I've taken. I've answered detailed questionnaires for her so she could know every detail I've taken in while on assignment. She's very observant. And as you say, she's had me watch the customers. I've learned that McCoy Stonewall

Enterprises is very interested in how the customer experience is."

"It is our most important objective. It has made us what we are today."

"I agree to a point, but if you don't mind me saying so, I believe that *you* are McCoy Stonewall Enterprises most important asset. You have an excellent eye for detail, all the way down to customer experience."

"You flatter me."

"I promise you it wasn't meant to flatter. It's just the truth as I see it."

She was a straight shooter and that made him all the more certain of what he was going to propose when the time was right.

"I'll check us in. We've got separate rooms, just so you know."

For an instant, he wished they had a suite so she would be closer to him. But that was not smart thinking on his part.

Still, as he walked toward the reservation desk, he knew he was looking forward to spending time with her.

He was not, however, looking forward to letting her in on the requirements of Granddaddy's will.

CHAPTER SIX

Amber stood back just a little as Morgan walked up to the desk and got their keys from the previously made reservations. She had a feeling that Mrs. Beasley had made the reservations. The receptionist was extremely nice. Of course, she couldn't imagine anyone not being nice to Morgan; he was very seriously handsome. She gave the young woman credit for not flirting with him. She was impressed with the receptionist's friendly but professional manner.

Obviously, someone had trained their people extremely well. Morgan would be pleased, because McCoy Stonewall Enterprises resorts were known for their people skills. The fact that he could buy a resort and retain the employees if they showed promise was a big plus. Not a lot of retraining involved.

She smiled when the receptionist welcomed her to the resort also. Then she went with Morgan to the elevator. It was a gorgeous hotel, with very sleek interiors and a wide porch that encircled the first floor, overlooking the iconic bay. The building was sleek and silver, with a lot of glass. She knew McCoy Stonewall Enterprises preferred lower-level facilities with great views and gorgeous resort grounds. This was different and she wondered what Morgan would decide during their time here.

When they were on the elevator, he handed her a key.

"I hope you like your room. Mrs. B sends her regards and says she thinks you'll enjoy it. I have made reservations for dinner at the restaurant on the top floor, overlooking the bay."

Amber hadn't brought anything really dressy.

"Don't look alarmed. I had Mrs. B send you something to wear since I didn't let you know this was part of the plan. Sorry about that."

He had thought of everything. Relief that she had something to wear to a fancy night out eased her worry. She couldn't help being curious about what Mrs. Beasley would have waiting for her. "Thank you for thinking of me. I'll admit I'm looking forward to dinner up there. It looks like it will be an amazing view. And the lights of Princeville will be beautiful, so thank you for asking me along on this trip. I'm here to help you in any way that I can."

He smiled. "I would expect nothing less of you. You've proved to be an extremely efficient assistant."

"I haven't really done anything. So, sadly, you can't make that assumption."

He laughed; the sound sent butterflies fluttering through her. "I guess I was thinking along the lines of what you did behind the scenes that I actually wasn't aware that you did but Mrs. Beasley was completely aware of all along. You wouldn't be here unless she thought you were the best. And I learned a long time ago to trust her."

"And so you keep telling me."

The elevator doors dinged then slid opened. They walked out into plush carpets of teal and gray. He anticipated beautiful rooms. He hadn't had Mrs. B book the most beautiful rooms but instead they had taken rooms that most of the resort guests would be staying in.

He glanced at Amber when they paused before turning left or right, depending on which room number they had. She was frowning.

"Are you upset?" he asked, concerned.

"No, I'm not upset. I'm just a little bit overwhelmed. This fabulous assistant that I am does tend to get overloaded on surprises. And it's been a very eventful and surprising day. I'll be ready to relax at dinner."

He smiled. "Then I'll be sure to let you relax. Here we are—this is your room. Mine is across the hall that way. I'll knock on your door in, say, an hour. Our reservations are for seven but I thought we would go and check out the terrace bar. You don't have to drink anything but if you want wine or whatever, you can. But since the guests enjoy it, we'll be checking it out."

"Thank you. I'll be ready. As long as I can fit into whatever Mrs. Beasley sent me."

He laughed. "And you doubt her?"

She smiled finally. "No, I don't. I'm actually anticipating finding out what is waiting for me in my room."

"You'll have to fill me in once I knock on your door. I'll be anticipating myself."

And with that, she passed her key over the door, opened it, and slipped inside.

Morgan strode to his room, his mind already thinking about the disaster that this evening could turn into. Once she heard what he was thinking of.

* * *

An hour later, when a light knock came on her door, Amber stared at her reflection in the full-length mirror. Apprehension burned in her gut as she took in her appearance.

The little black dress that had been waiting for her in her room, along with several other resort outfits that made her wonder how long they were going to be here, were all gorgeous and had to be unbelievably expensive. The dress fit perfectly, as if made for her. She hadn't realized that Mrs. Beasley had this particular strong point of being a personal assistant but the woman knew sizes and her taste was impeccable.

Amber had forced herself to leave her hair down although she normally, when working, pulled it back in a tight bun at her nape. After a bad experience with a boss early on in her career making herself as plain as possible had become a security measure for her. When her hair was down, she felt more vulnerable. After that first experience Amber had been very cautious with where she sent her resumes and with whom she chose to work. Everything had been fine, until, she'd been blindsided by this unhealthy admiration for her boss.

He's my boss.

The voice in her head yelled the warning but staring at herself in the mirror, she didn't feel at all like someone working for Morgan McCoy.

She felt like Cinderella transformed into a princess going to the ball.

And that was a very dangerous feeling for her.

She reminded herself this was simply dinner...a working dinner and nothing more. She turned and walked to the door on shaking legs. *She could not let herself forget that.* Taking a deep breath, she settled her hand on her stomach and willed the butterflies to just *please* fly away. And then she reached for the door and opened it.

A gasp nearly escaped her but thankfully she killed it with a hard swallow.

Morgan was a man to be reckoned with. Impeccable, just as she had envisioned him, standing in the hallway in a dark sports coat over a snowy-white shirt opened at the neck. He finished the look off with smoky-gray slacks with, surprisingly, what appeared to be expensive leather loafers that went with the casual effect of his dressy attire. The man surprised her once more. Mrs. Beasley had dressed Amber to match him.

Oh, what a night. She swallowed again, meeting his suddenly shadowed eyes. Eyes that for an instant had looked warm, hungry. *For her?*

No, she was mistaken and the warmth rushing through her was betraying.

What she'd thought she'd seen in those deep blue eyes couldn't be right. The man was not one who could be startled or surprised. And yet, he looked it.

His gaze drifted over her and then back up to her face and over her hair. She felt those eyes taking in every aspect of her. Unable to help herself, she lifted a hand to run down her hair.

"Is this okay?" she asked, her nerves getting the better of her.

"Yes. You look beautiful. Perfect." He cleared his throat and got that business expression back on his face and the startled expression of a man impressed was gone. "I see Mrs. B did her job well. We'll look like the perfect Hawaiian tourists dressed to have a great time."

"Yes, I agree. And might I add that you also look perfect." *Why had she said that?*

It might be true but it wasn't her right to say so.

As they went to the elevator, he let her pass in front of him and enter first. He followed, placing a hand possessively at the base of her back. Her pulse skittered dangerously and she felt as if she were in a convertible, rounding a curve at high speed. He pushed the button for the upper level, remaining close to her with his hand still on her back. She could breathe in his cologne, subtle spices mixed with deep tones of the scent of the sea…fresh, alluring, and it drew her as if she were pulled by the tide.

She marveled at the fact that he had looked so stunned for that brief moment.

Was it so startling to see her dressed up?

Now, as she slid her gaze to him, she caught him studying her hair. He had lingered so long on her hair and her face, it had made her almost wonder whether something had been wrong. But she couldn't worry about it; she wasn't the most gorgeous woman around but she could clean up nicely.

The doors opened to the restaurant. It was dazzling, with sparkling low-lit chandeliers and romantic candlelight flickering throughout the restaurant. The windows that circled around to match the entire resort with its circular build enabled almost every room to have a view of the ocean. He spoke to the hostess and she led them out on to the bar area on the patio to a secluded area near the end of the patio that had seating around a fire pit but also a table for two next to the balcony wall, overlooking the bay. Twinkle lights were everywhere; in a few places, there were more fire pits—very classy fire pits with couples gathered on the couches, some talking wildly and enjoying themselves and others snuggling. She had never in her wildest dreams envisioned that she would be in such a romantic place with Morgan. She had to remind herself again that she was, one, not his type and two, this was for business. But when he placed his hand on the small of her back once more and directed her toward one of the couches in the area near their table, she could easily have forgotten that this was not an intimate date.

Very easily have forgotten it.

CHAPTER SEVEN

He tried hard not to stare at Amber but it was impossible. She'd worn her hair down and not in that tight coiled knot. The dress Mrs. B had sent was stunning on her, and though tasteful, it was a far cry from the business attire she'd worn today and what he remembered her wearing in the office the time or two he now remembered seeing her. Until he saw her this morning with her hair pulled back, he hadn't even recognized her as the person he rescued the day before. But he had recognized her as the woman he'd seen a few times at the office. He told himself that he didn't have any right to like anything about Amber. But if he was going to offer her this contract, and he was, it was nice that he liked her. She made him laugh and that didn't happen often. And she challenged him in the brief time that they had known each other—at least twice.

"I'm glad you came with me. It's nice getting to know you better." And he had a feeling that this proposition that he was going to make to her tonight might actually or could actually ruin their working relationship, and maybe even anything else that they might be developing. They wouldn't be developing anything else—*where was his head?*

"Yes, well, thank you for bringing me. It seems I have a lot to thank you for on this trip. This is just breathtaking."

"I like the Princeville area, although I prefer the southern end. If you think that's breathtaking, you need to go to the canyon. You'll love it. Take a car one day and drive up there before we leave."

"I'll try, if there is time." She stood and moved to the railing.

He studied her from where he sat. He wanted to follow her to the railing and place a hand on either side of her and enjoy the view, with the scent of her sweet hair teasing him and the warmth of her body close to his. She turned and caught him watching her again. She caught him several times, but it was hard to keep his eyes off her. She tilted her head and studied him.

The expression on her face was quirky and made him smile. Again. "What?" he asked, feeling a little lighthearted suddenly. Morgan couldn't remember the last time he felt lighthearted.

"Do you have a plan for this visit or is the Mighty Morgan McCoy flying by the seat of his pants? I'm actually stunned if that's the case but, honestly, I can't figure anything else out."

"I might be flying by the seat of my pants. And I honestly can't remember the last time that happened. I fly by my gut a lot of times."

"Yes, I've heard that your gut makes a lot of your decisions—a lot of your big decisions."

He rose and moved to stand next to her. He turned his body to face her. Their hands that were hanging onto the ledge were almost touching. He suddenly had a very strong urge to take her hand in his like they had in the helicopter, except maybe not so tight.

"I look at the data, I take it in, and then I let my gut tell me which one. If the data is uncertain, especially. But I have been known to look at the data and go with my gut and it sometimes tells me not what the data says. I've learned that data isn't always right."

"I like that about you. People try to hem you into this certain persona. And I've found out that it's not exactly true. Not that I listen to office gossip. But there are times when it's hard not to hear things."

He grinned. "Now why is it that I never suspected that you listen to gossip? I take you as the type of person who does her job to the complete best of your ability and while on the job, you're so zeroed in on your job that you probably don't take time to listen to anything."

Her expression faltered. "I sound unbelievably boring when you put it that way." She didn't look happy.

He wanted to trace the line of her jaw and tell her he found her far from boring. He was fascinated by her and he wasn't even sure why. But he wanted to know more. "I don't know you well enough to make that judgment call. But I'm enjoying getting to know you.

I'm pretty boring, if you really look at my life."

It was true. He turned, put both elbows on the ledge and cupped his hands and studied the dark water down below.

She leaned close and said softly, "You've done a good job of putting up a barrier around yourself. No one would have any idea if you're boring or not. They just see a successful, somewhat of a loner, man."

He breathed her in. "You're very perceptive. I have my reasons for putting up walls."

"I'm sure you do. I can only imagine. Is it hard not letting people in?"

This woman—she had insight. "I let people in. Those who matter to me."

"That's good to know. Your family?"

"Yes, my brothers Wade and Todd. And I have some cousins I'm close to. Although we talk, I'm not there often. I did see them at my brothers' weddings, though. Well, at Wade's wedding. I think most of them were out of town for Todd's. But anyway, most of them know me."

"Well, I'm glad you have someone you can open up to."

"How about you? You asked me—now I'm asking you. Do you have anyone you open up to?"

She hesitated and that made him curious. "I-I have a friend," she said finally.

His spirits plummeted. "A boyfriend?" He had to ask that question. *Why hadn't he thought about that before now?*

"No, no boyfriend. I actually broke it off with my boyfriend about two years ago."

Something about the way she said that bit of information didn't sound right. "Really? Was there a problem?"

"Not a problem, except that I realized that I didn't love him and I refuse to marry anyone I don't love."

"That's a good plan to follow."

"Yes, I think so. Speaking of hopes and dreams, I'm still interested in why you asked me that earlier. Remember you were going to tell me why." Her brow crinkled. "I'm all ears when you want to expand on that odd statement."

"Do you want anything to drink?"

"Now you're using evasive tactics. I'm even more curious. What do you have up your sleeve, Mr.

Morgan McCoy?"

He waved his hand and called the waitress over. "I'll have a Canada Dry or ginger ale with lime—either one. Do you want anything?"

"I'll have the same. You don't drink?" she asked when the waitress moved away to get their order.

"I don't. I like being in control...at all times. I might have a glass of wine every once in a while." McCoy vineyards made an award-winning wine, thanks to his brother Todd and his dedication to the trade. "But for the most part, no, I don't drink." Certainly not now; he needed all of his faculties for what he was about to do.

"I don't either. I'm a control freak too."

He laughed. "I didn't call myself a freak and you certainly aren't."

She smiled, her pretty eyes dancing. His pulse raced and the thought that with her, he might have a hard time retaining his control.

"You haven't been around me long enough. One reason I am good at my job is my control tendencies. Mrs. Beasley and I are very much alike. I think she recognized that in me."

He studied her. She had no idea that a comparison of herself to Mrs. B was wrong. She didn't remind him of his sixty-year-old personal assistant in the least. Her gaze shadowed. She nibbled on her lip again; he had quickly learned it was a habit she had when she was deep in thought.

"You are in deep thought over there. Why don't you go ahead and say whatever's on your mind?"

"To be honest, I'm starting to get a little worried about this proposition you're going to tell me about." She bit her lip again.

It hit him like a sledgehammer. He frowned. "You think I'm going to proposition you? As in for—"

"I hope not." She broke him off before he put the offensive statement into words. "But it's crossed my mind, despite it not being something that I ever believed you would do."

Relief swept through him. "I wouldn't ever do that." He held her eyes with what he hoped she could see was clear honesty. "I would never disrespect you or any of my employees that way. I hope you know that."

She nodded. "I did…it was just something about how you spoke of this earlier. You seemed so conflicted."

The waitress dropped off their drinks and left. He picked his up and took a drink. The sweetness and carbonation burned down his dry throat.

The time was now. "Let's sit down over here and I'll tell you the whole sordid thing. But you have to agree to eat dinner no matter what you think about what I'm about to say. You have to agree that you'll hear me out, that you'll not get aggravated and leave me eating dinner alone."

She moved to sit on the cozy outdoor loveseat and he followed her. She set her drink down and then calmly crossed her arms and studied him intently. "Now you really have me intrigued. Maybe I should be worried but I'm actually not."

"I'm glad you're not worried, because I am. So, here's the deal."

Amber couldn't imagine what in the world Morgan was about to say. And she waited. The man looked nervous.

"As I said, my granddaddy passed away and I told

you that he left some pretty odd requirements in his will. It's not the easiest thing to share with just anyone, but the requirements require that I share them with someone. If I haven't chosen well...just bear with me. This is the most awkward and actually ridiculous thing I've had to ever deal with in my life. I loved my granddaddy but we butted heads all the time. He was one stubborn man, and I guess I was also one stubborn man. But I don't understand why he's putting me through this. Anyway, that's a needless conversation to go into because I can't get out of this. So, here's the deal. Until yesterday, I'm sorry, I hadn't actually really known you. And I'm guessing that I still don't really know you. But I'm a very good judge of character and that's why I'm going to put this out there for you. I feel I can trust you with the privacy that this requires. You can turn it down but if you would listen with an open mind, it will benefit you."

He paused, giving her time to answer, she presumed. She was so curious, she had to know what in the world he was talking about. "I'm listening."

"Okay, then here it is. My granddaddy raised my brothers and me after our father and our mother died in a plane crash, along with my uncle and my aunt. I am the man I am today because of my granddaddy. We are—were very much alike in personalities. Because of that, we didn't get along in the years before his sudden death."

She was riveted to his words as a flash of sorrow, swift and vibrant, filled his expression and she saw how much his granddaddy's death had affected—was still affecting—him. "I'm so sorry for your loss."

"Me too. But despite the fact that we butted heads, I loved him deeply and need to honor his memory. The only problem with that is…it turns out my granddaddy wanted great-grandchildren on the land he loved. That would be the ranch and the vineyards where Wade and Todd live. The resorts were a sidekick to him. They weren't the love of his life—that would be the ranch. And we three grandsons were busy building up the legacy that he was leaving us. The problem, obviously, was that none of us got married. None of us were even thinking about it when he died. He's a stubborn fella and he always got his way." He laughed, a bitter sound.

And with a hint of sadness, Amber noted. She had

the urge to reach out and cover his hand with hers but all the other things he was saying kept her from doing that. She was just going to sit here and listen.

"I'll just cut to the chase. My granddaddy gave each one of us three months to find someone to marry and then we have to be married for three months before we dissolve the marriage or divorce or whatever. He stipulated this in his will. Wade had to save the ranch, Todd had to save the vineyards, and I have to save the resorts. If any of us failed at our challenge, we all lost stakes in that division and it would be sold out from under us. After all the love and hard work Wade put into the ranch—it would have been gone, but he managed to do it. Todd loves the vineyard and he managed to save it. Both of them found wives and fulfilled their end of the will's stipulation. Now it's my turn. I've been a huge critic and knew it was coming. I've been sorely tempted to walk away, but my brothers did their part and if I don't go through with it, I'll never forgive myself."

"You'll lose the resorts?" She couldn't believe it. She stared at him, dumbfounded that his grandfather would do this. He didn't even have to tell her this is what the requirement was because she knew that Morgan put his entire being into these resorts.

"Exactly. So, there's my dilemma: the clock started ticking on my three months to find a bride. Not only did Granddaddy want us to get married but he built in a requirement of being married three months before he gave us the out of getting divorced and going on with our lives. We've decided we think he wasn't wanting to force us to get married; he hoped that in the process, we would fall in love and give him great-grandchildren. But he wasn't all ridiculous because he did give us a three-month out—which is the only reason I'm going through with this. I will be dissolving the marriage at the end of the three months. This will be strictly a marriage of convenience, a business deal and should be entered into as such."

She let his problem sink in. Her mind started whirling through what she would need to do to help him make this odd request happen. "You want me to help you find a wife? I've never had an assignment like this but I'll do my best. We will need to brainstorm the type of woman you're looking for, anyone you might have in mind and women with a reason they might marry for business."

Her brain had clicked into business mode and she was fully committed to the job. It was nothing like what she'd been envisioning, though the thought of him marrying, even for convenience, disturbed her. She wouldn't let herself dwell on that. She'd known from the beginning that her infatuation with him was purely a fantasy, and would never come true. She'd never stood a chance with the man. She cataloged what her next steps would be. She realized he was staring at her with a look of confusion on his handsome face, not a look he wore often.

"Is something wrong?" she asked, bringing her glass up and taking a sip of her drink.

"Yes, Amber. You've misunderstood. I'm proposing that *you* marry me."

"Me," Amber gasped, sucking ginger ale down her windpipe, and choked.

CHAPTER EIGHT

"Excuse me?" Amber rasped.

Morgan moved closer to her and patted her between the shoulder blades. "I'm sorry, didn't mean to choke you up. Are you okay?"

She nodded, swallowed hard, and faced him. Her eyes narrowed in what looked like disbelief. "I'm fine but *what* did you say?"

He gave her a gentle pat on the shoulder, not wanting to pull his hand away but doing so anyway. "I'm asking you if you would consider marrying me? It would be a contractual agreement with a prenuptial agreement that would compensate you very well for the three months. We can go over the specifics but you would be paid extremely well. The catch is that after the wedding, we would have to live together for three months at my home on the ranch in Texas. There's no requirements about us even sharing a room, so you can relax on that. And at the end of the three months, we would get a very quick and easy divorce."

She just stared at him. Not blinking.

He kept talking, completely out of his element in this moment. He had never felt this raw and stupid, really. She probably thought he was losing his mind to ask her. "You could go your way with a significant settlement package from the company, too—you would be able to use it to do anything you wanted. That's why I asked you if you had any hopes or desires or dreams, any needs because that's all I have to offer you. I really need your help. And I'm making a mess of this but to be honest, this is the most unimaginable contract I've ever had to negotiate in my life. It is very awkward. I'm not comfortable with it at all. But my granddaddy wasn't worrying about my comfort when he concocted this scheme." He ran a hand over his hair and then cupped his neck as he squinted at her. The woman could play poker with the best there was in Las Vegas. "Okay, I'm going to need you to say something. Or slap me. But do something."

* * *

Amber was stunned speechless. She inhaled deeply, praying for calm as she fought to gather her thoughts. She had to say something. "I don't mean to be rude, but was your grandfather insane?"

His lips twitched at the edges. "No, but I asked a similar question at the reading of the will. I was assured that he was fully functioning at the time of his death."

"I guess that's good to know. Still…I just met you. I mean, yes, I have worked for you but as far as actually talking to you and having a conversation with you, I just crossed into that territory." She paused as dawning occurred to her. "Oh, goodness." It hit her hard and strong that Morgan McCoy had saved her life. *I owe him.* She put her hand to her forehead, closed her eyes, and let it sink in. "Oh my gosh, I owe you. You're calling in the favor. You saved my life—now I must marry you."

"*No.*" His reaction was volatile; he cupped a hand over hers and held on. "Not at all. I would never do that. It never even crossed my mind." He looked fierce. "I haven't even thought of that. Please don't think that at all. Amber, I'm asking you this because you're very dedicated to your job. You are obviously very trustworthy and talented. Your integrity is evident just in the little time I've known you today. You are all out to do your job well, even after going through what you did yesterday. You just got out of the hospital this morning after you almost drowned yesterday. And you were committed to getting your job done today. That's dedication to the extreme. But also, you don't mind challenging me—to be honest, I've enjoyed being around you. So, my thinking was you might do this to help with a dream you might be able to fulfill afterward. And for selfish reasons on my part—I feel if I have to go through this, it would be nice to be around someone I like."

She blinked hard, touched and bothered at the same time by his declaration. *He wasn't calling in an IOU.* But as she sat there and looked at him, she couldn't shake the realization that she did owe him. If he hadn't saved her, she wouldn't be here right now.

She would be dead.

The realization slapped her in the face—she owed him and the least she could do was give him three months of her life. A life she wouldn't have if it weren't for him. "I need to process this."

"Believe me, I understand. I'm still processing it. My granddaddy knew how to get to me. He definitely knew. He knew it would be hardest on me. I guess I thought that all along there would be a disclaimer in there that if one of my brothers got married, he wouldn't require it of the others. But no, that release was not in the will. He knew that he was going to do this to me."

She realized that he was still holding her hands and the butterflies that had been in her stomach earlier shifted and began to flutter. "I will need to think about this overnight. Do I have a timeline?"

"Umm, no, but tomorrow would be fine. If you turn me down, I have to go find someone else because I will not lose McCoy Stonewall Hotel and Resort Division of McCoy Stonewall Enterprises. If you look at the contract and you want more money, I will up the price."

"No, I'm not thinking about the money. I'm sure whatever you've written down on that is plenty of compensation. I know how you operate. I'm just processing."

"Well then, let's have dinner. I told you to relax and then I sprung this on you before you even had time to eat, so that's why I wanted you to agree to not run out of here screaming that I was a crazy man."

"I think dinner would be a good idea. And after I relax just a smidgeon, I might have some questions for you." She stared out over the barely lit bay. The lights shimmered on the water and the boats. It looked tranquil and so completely out of touch with the turmoil rolling inside her.

It was the first sunset that she was seeing after almost dying. It was beautiful and it was a very stark reminder that whatever Morgan said about not owing him, she did.

And then there was the crush. That part of the equation could get awkward. Very, very awkward.

* * *

They managed to make it through most of the meal with small talk, though tension stretched between them. He had expected a quick refusal and maybe even a resignation. Instead, she was thinking it over. And he was giving her space to do that, following her lead. When she was ready to talk about it again, he would give her any and all the information he could.

They ate their gourmet meals, discussing the food and the service, which was all perfect. They were both impressed with the place and now, to have something to focus on other than the obvious question between them, they focused on how all the others around them seemed to be enjoying the restaurant. They, too, appeared to love it.

All the while, he was thinking of Amber's thoughts. He couldn't imagine that she would be thinking it over, but she had never answered his question about her hopes and dreams and maybe money could help her fulfill a wish. Or a need.

The candlelight flickered between them now that the sun had gone down. The night faded to black, bringing with it the twinkle of lights all around them. Any other evening, it would have been romantic. The fact that they were mulling over his very unromantic proposal hindered that, but he kept finding himself thinking about how beautiful she was and how pleased he was that she was considering his offer.

"Would you like dessert? Maybe some cheesecake? Or that house specialty looks good," he asked as the waitress removed their plates and had asked whether they wanted a dessert menu.

"No, thank you." She paused. "Wait, aren't we supposed to be checking out everything?"

He laughed, easily, something he noticed. "Yes, we are. What if I order cheesecake and the house special? That chocolate thing really looks good."

"Perfect. And we can taste both. Plus, black coffee."

"I like the way you think. Black—no cream or sugar?"

"None." She smiled.

He motioned for the waitress, made the order, and found Amber watching him with assessing eyes.

"I could get used to this trying out resorts for a living," she said. "Do you normally travel alone?"

"You're good at it and yes, I normally travel alone. Mrs. B had come on this trip because of this deal. But as you know, she is usually at the office." For the first time ever, he thought about how having a companion along might make traveling even better. "I love traveling and I used to see the sights while I was visiting places. But it's gotten to where now, I just work." His mind wandered, thinking about how his life had twisted and turned and changed over the years. This hotel resort chain was his life and he loved it. He never really let himself think about life any other way, not after Shannon. He pushed the thought of her out of his brain. "I'm glad you're here."

"I am too, even if it was or has been the oddest trip of my life. Could have been the last trip of my life…"

He impulsively reached across the table and covered her hand with his, hoping to comfort her. "I hope it ends up being the best trip of your life that you've had so far and that you decide to help me out."

Her gaze dropped to their hands and she bit her lip…his insides coiled as he waited for her answer.

"Here you go," the waitress said, breaking the moment. He let go of Amber's hand as she set the desserts on the table, between them. Then she stepped to the side as the waiter who had come with her set the two cups of coffee in front of them. After making sure they had what they needed, they were left alone again. But the moment was gone.

"This looks delicious." Amber pointed her fork at the chocolate delicacy. "I can't help it—I'm a woman and the cliché is that we all love chocolate. But I also like cheesecake, so I'm going to enjoy this."

He watched as she dipped her fork into the very rich and very moist-looking cake covered in chocolate shavings. It really looked delicious. She placed the fork in her mouth and then slowly pulled it out. He decided he might want to try that too.

"This is to die for." She closed her eyes, letting the cake melt in her mouth, he assumed.

Whatever she was doing, he got his fork. He needed some cake to help with the odd nerves that were tightening his insides.

"On that note, I'm going to have to try this." He dipped his fork into the chocolate, got a good portion, and took a bite. *Oh, yes.* "Umm, I would say on this dessert alone that this place gets five stars." It was really great. Just as good as she made it look.

"I have a feeling we're going to not do what we said."

He was getting a second forkful. "Oh, yeah, and what is that?"

"We aren't going to be able to just take a bite." She dipped her fork into the end of it where there was more of the chocolate icing and took the bite.

He didn't close his eyes because he was too busy watching her. The only thing better was watching how much she liked it. She could make a commercial eating the cake and sell boatloads of the stuff.

She could probably sell anything to him at the moment.

She opened her eyes and he grinned at her. He felt lighthearted—it was a strange feeling. A nice feeling. "I think we had a good idea and I, for one, think we need to knock off the rule thing and just enjoy this. Which, I'm going to say, you are definitely enjoying it."

She laughed. Her eyes twinkled. "Well, you know, that is what I'm here for—to test things out. And this is heavenly."

They both ate another couple of bites and then she set her fork down and picked up her coffee mug and took a long, slow sip. "They make good coffee, too. I love black coffee after sweet cake."

"I have to say, I've never been around many women who like black coffee."

"I know, I know. I hear that all the time. I just like it black. I have to say, I don't drink a lot of coffee, contrary to a lot of my friends. But when I do, I like it with the sweet. You know, the two kind of go together, therefore if I don't want to eat a lot of dessert, I don't drink a lot of coffee—one cup in the morning, maybe one in the afternoon. And then maybe one in the evening with dessert if I'm celebrating or doing my job. Speaking of which, if this is a part of my job, I will gladly keep it for as long as you want to keep me."

"Done."

She studied him over the edge of the coffee mug. Her pretty eyes turned serious. "Do you—well, I guess I'm going to get a little bit personal here because you did ask me to marry you. But do you travel with someone? Do you have a friend, a girlfriend who goes with you? I'm assuming you don't since you're not marrying her, or you had a girlfriend and she turned you down, which, if that's the case, I'm sorry."

"And again, I mean, that's why I like you—you're very straightforward; you don't pull any punches. I'm all for that. No, I don't have a girlfriend. I don't have a friend; I don't have anyone who travels with me. I normally travel alone, especially since my wife's death. It's just the way I prefer it. I do date on occasion. I do have friends all over the world. But nothing since my first marriage has ever been serious and I guess it's easy to say I'm basically married to my job now."

Her expression grew pensive, as if she had questions but wasn't sure whether to ask them. If it was about his marriage he didn't want to go any deeper into that.

She took a breath. "And you like it that way? You don't get lonely?"

"Like I say, I have dinner with female friends all over the place. I have business friends everywhere. And I go home every once in a while. I talk to my brothers once a week when possible, and once a month when we have an online conference meeting. I enjoy my work." He sounded slightly defensive, even to himself. And he was.

She took a sip of her coffee. "If I marry you, when will I see you? Do I continue to work at the office while we have this arrangement? I guess I'm a bit confused. If your grandfather made this requirement for you, and he knows how you work, then how does three months make a difference?"

"That's where the ranch comes into play. Granddaddy is, *was...*" He paused, still finding it hard to believe he was gone. "J.D. was a very cunning and astute businessman, and man in general, who knew what he wanted and how best to get it. The deal is for the three months that I'm married I, we, have to go home to my house at the ranch and live there. Not just visit."

"You have a house at the ranch?"

"I do. I built it several years ago. It's not up by the main house, but farther back into the property. I never stay there much. But for the three months that I'm married, I have to live in my home on the property. I can be gone no more than a week out of the three months. My brothers stipulations were they could be gone one week each month, but my granddaddy changed the stipulation on me. He wants me and my temporary wife in Stonewall basically full time. So the deal is, I'll work from home and if you marry me, you can assist me from home. Or, when you're not assisting me, you're free to explore and enjoy Stonewall. It's near Fredericksburg." He didn't elaborate. She was from Texas; she knew that the Texas Hill Country area was beautiful in its own rugged way. "The ranch is beautiful and the vineyard is, too. I'm sure Allie and Ginny, my brothers' wives, will be happy to spend time with you."

"And how about you? You won't be happy to spend time with your new bride?"

Yes. He frowned, nervous at her question. "Well, it is a business deal. I would need you to go into it with that thought."

Her delicate chin lifted. "Okay. Look, I know I'm not your type. You've said you have women to go to dinner with all over the world and I'm sure they are gorgeous, amazing women. But you are asking me to marry you because I'm efficient, I'm straightforward and I guess that's the requirements for the position and you think I have integrity. I guess the integrity is so that I accept the terms of the agreement and I leave without any mess in the end. Am I right?"

He felt very uncomfortable about what she was saying. "That's not exactly it. Yeah, that's true about the efficient and integrity, but you're beautiful. Why would you not think you're beautiful? However, I'm not basing this on looks—I'm basing this on the person."

She looked down, and he wanted to tell her she was as beautiful as any woman he'd ever met, much less ever taken to dinner. But he didn't.

She looked up in that minute and caught him staring. "I wasn't fishing for a compliment, I promise you. I'm just trying to get a feel for what I'm getting myself into. And I'm wondering why you would even enter into an agreement like this with someone who doesn't even stand a chance of becoming the real Mrs. Morgan McCoy?"

He balked. "This was a very delicate situation. I think you just asked me a question that I'm not completely sure how to answer."

"Please, take your time. I'm in no rush for the

answer. I'm trying the cheesecake."

There was an edge to her voice. *Was she aggravated?* She took a sip of the coffee. It hit him then; he had *insulted* her. "Amber, I offered this position because I trust you. I'm not planning to marry anyone for real ever again."

"I see."

"I'm not going to lie—yes, that's part of it. You are convenient and you have all the qualifications that make you a good candidate for the position. I'm not sure where you get what my type is, but I'm not getting into that. I might be able to fall for you." *What was he saying?* "What I mean is, this is cut-and-dry— you know what you're getting when we split and I know what I'm getting when we split. There's no complication there. That's what I'm saying. This is already complicated enough without complicating it more."

"I see. Well…" She took a bite of the cheesecake.

He watched her savor the bite of cheesecake as she pulled it off the fork with closed lips. Only she didn't close her eyes this time. She watched him. And he watched her. And he wondered what he was getting himself into. Because he knew that there was something different about her that, yes, attracted him. But this being simpler made it all better.

"Morgan, I may regret this," she said at last. "But I can't help myself. You go by your gut and I'm going to go by my gut, and I'm going to say yes to your proposal."

"You are?" His heart pounded and he wasn't sure he'd heard her correctly. He hadn't been expecting this. She had said she was going to think about it. "You said you were going to think about it," he repeated like an idiot. He was totally taken off guard.

"I know I did and that's what I thought. But, you know, your grandfather really intrigues me. I want to see your ranch, and let's just get the elephant out of the way right now. I do have hopes and dreams like you asked me, and knowing right up front that I'm not a person you would fall for keeps my headspace clear. I mean, in the end, when I walk away—no mess and no squabble and no fireworks of any kind—I'll have a wonderful nest egg to open my own business."

"And that is?"

She smiled gently, with a sudden faraway look in

her eyes. "I'd like to start a nonprofit to help people with struggling businesses to have consultations with successful business owners in their field. My specialty would be marketing, but I could bring in women or men from all backgrounds to offer their services. I've never really thought I could find a way to actually start it. So, I think I would be an idiot not to take you up on your offer."

And that was it—clean, concise just like he wanted it... *Then why did it feel so wrong?*

CHAPTER NINE

Amber woke the next morning not able to believe what she had consented to. But she had been unable to not do it. She was too curious, though she was insulted that he had basically told her that he didn't want to fall in love with her or couldn't fall in love with her. *Was she crazy?* She had done it anyway and she told herself that if she was thinking that she was going to try to make a liar out of him and make him fall in love with her, then, yes, she needed to be committed because it was a terrible idea.

But she liked him. Before this trip, she had an infatuation with him, but she liked how he was handling this crazy idea of his grandfather's. She couldn't help but think that his grandfather must have loved him very much, not that Morgan realized it at the moment. But she thought that his grandfather cared deeply for him because she saw exactly what his granddaddy saw: a man who worked all the time, a man who probably didn't seem like he had any close friends other than his brothers, and a man who just couldn't keep that up. His grandfather was trying to give him a chance, though he was minimizing the chance that he could actually find someone to marry him on this weird idea and fall in love at the same time.

She had decided while sitting there that this was her shot. She could watch him marry someone else or she could actually take this time and see whether she had a chance with him. It was her best shot and if she didn't risk it, she was probably going to regret this for the rest of her life. She just couldn't say no. She was stepping out on a wing and a prayer, and going to see what came next.

She wasn't a gold digger; she didn't care about the money. She was just intrigued by the man. Morgan was driven but he was lonely, she thought. He was amazing; he was fascinating to her and she wanted to get to know him better. She wanted to see who he was on this ranch where he had built a home and never went to it.

She stretched in the bed when there was a knock on her door. She picked up the white robe on the end of her bed, put it on, and went to the door, wondering who was there. It was seven o'clock. Oh, goodness, she needed to get up and get dressed. The dinner had been late and he had told her he had business to do this morning and not to worry about meeting him until nine. She opened the door; a waiter with a rolling tray stood there. She blinked.

"Room service."

"I didn't order room service."

He looked at the list. "Mr. Morgan did."

She stepped back, smiling. "Thank you. Then by all means, bring it in." He brought it in and she went to her purse to pull out a tip.

He held his hand up. "No, ma'am, that's already been taken care of. But enjoy your meal." And then he left.

Feeling slightly enthusiastic at the thought of having breakfast in bed basically, she walked over and lifted the lid on the trays. There was an assortment of pastries; there was bacon and eggs and fruit and coffee and orange juice. And there was cheesecake. Smiling, she lifted the last lid and found a huge piece of chocolate cake. The man had a sense of humor.

She took the coffee to the bedside table and poured herself a cup. Then she took the plate with the chocolate cake on it and a fork, and climbed back into bed. She took a big bite of the cake then a sip of coffee... *Oh, yes, this was heaven.*

She was getting herself into a crazy situation and at this moment she wasn't even worried she might have a problem. Her phone rang and she picked it up. "Hello."

"Good morning, Amber. This is Mrs. Beasley. I hear that congratulations are in order."

"Good morning. You've talked to Mr. McCoy, I mean Morgan?"

There was a chuckle on the line. "I have indeed. And I've arranged or will be arranging for a wedding tomorrow evening on the beach. Just a small affair, but I think we need to have a nice little gathering. Would you like to go shopping tomorrow morning for something to wear?"

"Mrs. Beasley, it—" She halted, not knowing whether to tell her it wasn't real. *Or did Mrs. Beasley know the truth?* "That sounds fun. Yes, thank you. I'll have breakfast and be ready whenever you're ready. Are you feeling up to it?"

"I feel fantastic. Never felt better. I guess whatever was wrong with me got better last night. I'm looking forward to it. You know, I don't have any children of my own, so going wedding dress shopping with you will be a wonderful treat."

"Thank you."

"I'll meet you at the car in the morning at nine."

"Perfect." She hung the phone up and set the chocolate cake down. *What had she gotten herself into?* Mrs. Beasley hadn't sound surprised at all. That was odd. Very odd.

Her phone rang again. She picked it up and saw it was Morgan. Her heart pounded as she answered his call. "Good morning," she said, and was answered with a chuckle. The sound sent ripples of awareness through her. She was in trouble and she knew it. *Too late now.*

"Good morning to you. Did you enjoy breakfast?"

She smiled. "I had chocolate cake and it was as good this morning as it was last night. Thank you."

He chuckled. "I think you might have started something for the future, Mrs. Soon-to-be- McCoy."

His words sank in. "It's still hard to believe. Speaking of, I just got a call from Mrs. Beasley and she's asking me if I want to go shopping for wedding dresses. Or something suitable to wear at a beach wedding. Did you know we were getting married at a beach wedding tomorrow evening?"

"I actually asked her to set it up. I know it's only for three months but we do have to put on a little bit of a show. People in the office will wonder."

"Yes, I understand that. Did Mrs. Beasley sound surprised at all this morning when you called her?"

"Not at all. She told me that she thought you would be the perfect person to marry me. See, she knows what's in my grandfather's will. And she evidently planned this."

"You're kidding me? *Mrs. Beasley*?"

"She thought that when I actually met you, I would see what she saw in you. She thinks very highly of you. I can't say that enough—she really does. And so, you've been basically handpicked by Mrs. B."

"That is just too strange."

"I hope that doesn't mean you're going to back out because she realized what might happen before we did."

"No, I'm not going to back out. I gave you my word and already agreed. It would have to be something very terrible to make me back out."

"And that's exactly what I thought you would say."

"So I'm about to go looking for a dress because I didn't bring anything for romantic evenings where I'm asked to be the wife of my boss and I didn't bring a dress to marry my boss in. Imagine that."

"How about some jeans or shorts?"

"Yes, I brought a pair. And Mrs. Beasly also had some sent when she sent me that beautiful dress. She thought of everything."

"She always does. I'm wondering if you're ready to head out soon."

"Sure, certainly. Have you gotten everything here that you came for?"

He paused. "I actually got everything I need. We'll

be busy tomorrow with getting ready for the wedding, small and intimate. I still want you to have some pampering and to pick out the dress you want. So, I wanted to take you somewhere today. If you can handle a ride back to the resort today."

"I can." She would, even if it killed her.

"Good. Meet me downstairs at ten."

After agreeing she hung up, brimming with curiosity.

"Where are we going?" Amber stared at the black Jeep on the side of the road as the helicopter lowered to the dry field on the southern end of Kauai.

"You'll find out soon." He squeezed her hand and smiled at her. She'd made the trip better, clinging to his hand after he'd offered it. He had to admit that he enjoyed her holding his hand. He told himself that it was okay to like her. She was easy to like.

Her eyes were bright as she looked back at him. "You like surprising people."

"I guess I like surprising you. You are, after all, basically saving my dreams." And she was. She'd said at dinner the night before that she owed him. But the truth was he owed her and knowing that made him want to give her things. And he knew she would enjoy the magnificent drive up to view Waimea Canyon.

When the chopper landed and the blades were off, he helped her out of the helicopter and then, continuing to hold her hand, he led her across the dry, crusted land to the waiting Jeep. The driver opened the door and he helped her climb inside; then he went around and climbed behind the wheel.

"Buckle up. Here we go."

She looked around at the desert-looking area they'd been dropped off at. "This looks nothing like Princeville with its lush greenery. I can't get over the different looks of this island."

He pulled out onto the road. "It is amazing. And we're heading to the canyon. That, too, is different. The colors of the canyon walls are vibrant reds and golds, and the dirt is so red it looks like cayenne pepper."

"I'm excited. I really wanted to come after you told me about it but I wasn't looking forward to doing it alone."

He had never come with anyone before and it had been a while since he'd driven it. He turned onto the road that would wind its way up to the lookouts and enjoyed looking over and seeing her pretty dark hair being tousled by the wind around her smiling face.

They stopped several times, just because she wanted to get out and look at the dirt that mounded on the sides of the road with wildflowers sticking out in some places.

By the time they'd made it to the lookout over the canyon, there was a rainbow spanning the canyon. It was perfect.

"It's gorgeous." She spun to look at him, her expression one of ecstatic joy as her eyes danced with emotion. She held her phone up. "We have to take a picture of the two of us with the canyon and the rainbow behind us." She moved close to him, placing herself slightly in front of him. He wrapped a hand around her waist, feeling her hip bone. She held her arms up, the phone aimed at them. She stood on her tiptoes to bring her face closer to his and catch the canyon behind them. He tightened his hand around her, holding her close so she could get the shot.

She smelled like sweet vanilla and he thought of

cookies.

"Look at the camera and smile." She laughed as he did as he was told and she snapped the selfie shot.

"Would you like me to take another one for you?" a young woman asked as she passed by with a group.

"Would you? That would be great." Amber handed her the camera and then, to his surprise, she turned toward him and placed her hand on his heart. "Smile again," she said and he did.

But then she looked up at him and all he could think about was kissing her. He had his arm around her and fought off the want to wrap his other arm around her and kiss her long and hard. For the blink of an eye, they stared into each other's eyes; something electric wrapped around them and bound them there.

She blinked and then, as if finding a strength he wasn't able to find, she stepped away to take the phone and thank the young woman for taking their photo.

Morgan had to shake himself to get his mind back on safer ground.

Because he was beginning to realize that this marriage might not be as easy as he'd believed it would be.

CHAPTER TEN

Amber didn't realize there were so many higher-end dress shops on the small island but they were in Princeville, with many more high-end shops and hotels. To her surprise, Mrs. Beasley knew everywhere to go. She was realizing that Mrs. Beasley was just a wealth of information. The woman knew her business in the office and she knew her business out of the office. If her boss asked her about anything, she had thoroughly researched it. The woman was amazing. They went to two shops that were extremely expensive and even though Mrs. Beasley kept assuring her that it was fine—that she had Morgan's executive platinum credit card and his assurance that the sky was the limit—Amber just couldn't go there. It wasn't her.

Finally, she asked Mrs. Beasley to take her somewhere at least in the middle of the price range and they ended up in a lovely store. It was in a very touristy area but they had beautiful evening attire for anyone, especially geared for tourists who might be coming to the island for a destination wedding. It was perfect and she spied several white dresses the moment she walked in the door.

"Mrs. Beasley, this is the right store. I don't know what the prices are but I can see the dresses are gorgeous and they're light. They're not officially wedding dresses but they're island evening attire. Even though we haven't spoken about it since we got together, Morgan told me that you know about the agreement."

Mrs. Beasley's eyes twinkled. "Yes, I know about the agreement and I have reason to believe that you fit perfectly. Am I wrong?"

Her breath caught in her lungs. "No, you weren't wrong. But I have to remember that this is a business deal."

"Yes, dear, you must remember that or you could get your heart broken, correct?"

She stared at Mrs. Beasley. The woman looked as if she could read Amber's innermost thoughts, her heart. But surely not. Amber scanned back through her memory, trying to think whether she had ever in any way given away that she was infatuated with her boss. *Infatuated*, not in love. In the office, she had very little, if no, contact with him but they were in visual contact sometimes; he just hadn't ever noticed her. And there were reasons for that, since she wore her hair so strictly pulled back in a tight knot and she wore very professional large glasses that for some reason she had always used to hide behind. And she wore very conservative, very muted tones. Among all the women in the office, she stood out the least.

Not that Morgan ever really noticed much but business in the office. Had she somehow given away that she was crazy about her boss? She didn't think so. Mrs. Beasley was just making a wild guess. "My heart won't get hurt."

Mrs. Beasley tilted her head to the side and assessed her with serious eyes. "Well, I hope that you don't say that lightly or that you don't say that too strongly, either. I've always found that it's wise to keep yourself open to possibilities. There's a world of possibilities out there, even the possibility of a personal assistant marrying her boss for strange and odd reasons and it turning into a fairy-tale romance and true love."

"Mrs. Beasley, do you even know what you're encouraging me to think about?"

"Oh, yes, I know very well what I'm trying to encourage you to think about. I have been with Morgan McCoy for years. I would never tell him this unless he asked, but I adore him. I think he is a fabulous, fabulous man and I, like his grandfather, who I knew before him, wish only the best for him. And I'm just making clear to you that I, and I'm sure his grandfather would, approve of you. I think that you could make him a fantastic wife for the long haul, as we would say. And I don't want you to completely dismiss that possibility."

A swirl of emotions erupted inside Amber. Her knees weakened at the very idea that Mrs. Beasley truly did believe she was right for this position. And that the woman had very carefully chosen her.

"Mrs. Beasley, I don't want to disappoint you, but I'm just going to caution you to not get your hopes up. Morgan has made it quite clear that this is strictly a business deal. I think you should know that. And I'm going to strive very hard not to cross that line. I have to live with myself after this. At the end of three months, I will walk away, without any hype or fuss, just as we have talked about together. No conflict, no problems for him or his company. No problems of the heart is included also, and I think that is what he meant most of all. He doesn't want things complicated."

"Well, we shall see. But right now, we need to find you that dress so you can get back and sign all that frivolous paperwork that I had to help get together in a massive hurry this morning while you were having that luscious breakfast."

He had sent breakfast to her again that morning. "Oh, did you order my breakfast this morning and yesterday?"

"Yes, and wasn't it fabulous? Morgan called me first thing yesterday morning and told me to order breakfast for you. I was to go all out and especially order cheesecake and chocolate delight or supreme or whatever that chocolate dish was I put on the order for you. And black coffee."

Disappointment rushed through her. She had believed he had ordered her breakfast. It was a silly disappointment but it was still there. "I see. I thought Morgan ordered that for me."

Mrs. Beasley's eyes twinkled again. "Oh, you did? And you liked the idea that he ordered that for you?"

What had she just done? She'd given herself away. *Doggone, what was wrong with her?* "Well, yes, but don't get the wrong idea about that. It was just nice that he had remembered and it was a nice gesture. Thank you for ordering it."

"I was just doing my job. If he hadn't called me and asked me to make the request, it wouldn't have happened. You especially wouldn't have gotten cheesecake and chocolate cake for breakfast."

This was true. But still, she could admit to herself that for some reason she would have felt more special if he had actually picked up the phone and called in the order to the desk. *And why was she worried about it being special?* She needed to keep her head on straight. And not get carried away, especially over a room service breakfast. She was going to have to really watch herself because ridiculousness did not have any place in this relationship. She had to keep her head and her heart on straight.

And that meant starting now. "I think I'll try that dress right there first," she said as a saleswoman approached them with a big smile.

"Ah, that's a great choice."

They walked around the room and quickly gathered up several beautiful white tropical-type dresses. But the one she had chosen first was her favorite and when she tried it on, she felt like it was the dress. It was off the shoulder, with a straight torso that fanned out to a flowing skirt that went just below mid-calf and had a white strap across one shoulder. It had a very sedate and tasteful look but it also had a flowing, flirty feel that she adored.

She tried on several others—some of them a bit more party-ish, some of them more white, extremely sedate—but she kept coming back to the first one. The twinkle in Mrs. Beasley's eye told her that was the one she liked too. She came out of the dressing room one last time with the dress on again. "What do you think?

This is my favorite."

"I'm so glad you chose that one. Mine too. And I think Morgan's going to love it also, which is very important."

She wanted to reiterate to Mrs. Beasley not to press that but the woman had made up her mind that she was excited about this and the possibilities that could unfold in the future for Morgan and Amber. Amber thought of the pictures on her phone that the young woman had taken the day before. She had captured that magic moment when Amber had been in his arms, with the Waimea Canyon and the rainbow behind them. But she had also caught them staring at each other just before she shook herself from an insane moment of hope and wishful thinking, thinking that he, too, was thinking love was possible.

She'd moved out of his embrace immediately, but it was captured on camera forever.

* * *

Morgan held Amber's hands and looked at her as the preacher recited the traditional wedding vows. *Why hadn't he changed them?* For all intents and purposes, it really didn't matter. And yet, when the preacher asked him if he would *love and cherish her, in sickness and in health, until death do you part,* it made him very uncomfortable with the whole situation. And yet, he went through with it anyway.

But looking at her and the trusting look in her eyes, he felt a protectiveness over her that startled him. He tried to block all the emotions that had suddenly derailed him and gritted his teeth to refrain from getting any more emotional connection to this wedding.

They signed papers an hour before the ceremony that had disclosed everything and made it completely legal and fair. They would dissolve the marriage in three months, quickly and easily. And they would go their separate ways.

And then they would start over and if he chose later to remarry, then it would be with true vows. But as she recited her vows to him, he could imagine being with Amber for life. He had never imagined anything like that would ever happen to him again. He was happy with his life now; even though there might have been some small discontent and regret sometimes, he kept reminding himself that not many people had the opportunity that he had. He loved his work. And not having to worry whether his wife married him for love or money gave him peace of mind. He wouldn't forget that.

As she looked up at him, Amber's eyes shadowed, seconds before they cleared. If she had also momentarily lapsed into thinking emotionally or more romantically about this situation, she wasn't now. It was for the best. He squeezed her hands slightly but she did not squeeze back. A small smile came to her lips; however, it didn't touch her eyes.

That worried him but then the preacher announced them husband and wife.

"You may kiss your bride."

Morgan looked at the preacher; he nodded and smiled encouragement. Mrs. B, who was their only witness, clapped her hands once and he thought she might have murmured "aw" or something like that. But mostly he was thinking that he had to kiss Amber now. Something inside him warned him if he kissed Amber, he might be in a danger zone.

"Kiss your bride," the preacher urged him.

With his pulse racing, he gently pulled Amber toward him. She hesitated; her eyes flashed panic before she blinked hard and it was gone. He took her in his arms and then lowered his lips to hers.

The world spun around him. He tightened his arms, forgetting everything as her trembling lips met his and her arms slid around his neck as he bent her backward, driven to get as close to her as he could possibly get. He felt her hands tighten into fists, gathering his shirt tightly. Sanity filtered into his thoughts and he lifted his lips a breath away from hers. But her hands didn't release him; her eyes were closed, her dark lashes black against her soft, golden skin.

Pulled by a desire he'd never felt before, he kissed her again, long and slow. Her lips were warm and receiving, and she might have gasped when he had come back in for the second kiss. With strength he had to fight for, he pulled away at last. Their eyes met and hers were raw with emotions, alive with vivid blues he wanted to dive into…the light went out of her eyes in an instant and shuttered. She let go of him and he did the same, feeling as if something precious had just gone out.

CHAPTER ELEVEN

They flew home on the jet. Morgan was an odd combination of business and kindness and it struck her that he was trying really hard to be kind to her, while also keeping her at arm's length. She understood it. The ceremony had blown her away. Emotions that she hadn't wanted to feel nor had she expected to feel completely overwhelmed her during the ceremony. And the kiss had sent her world spinning.

She reminded herself once again that she barely knew him. She had not fallen for the man. She was misplacing feelings of gratitude for him having saved her life.

That was it.

Mrs. Beasley had chosen to fly home on another plane—first class, of course, paid for by Mr. Morgan McCoy and his platinum-plated credit card. She had insisted that he and Amber needed time together, as if this were a real wedding. Amber didn't know what to do about Mrs. Beasley's misplaced excitement about the marriage.

Sitting in the creamy leather seat of the plane, she watched the clouds go by as they flew over the ocean toward Texas. Morgan was working on his computer. She had work to do also and spent time on her computer finishing up some files she'd been working on before the trip. They spoke off and on but worked mostly in silence.

It was a long plane flight; thankfully, some of it would be spent sleeping.

She closed her computer and studied him. He closed his too and they smiled at each other. Awkwardness filled the space between them.

They had both changed into casual wear. He looked nice in his more casual slacks and his boots again. She wondered whether he ever wore jeans. She wondered what he looked like, growing up as a cowboy on a ranch. She realized she wanted to see that side of him. It was one of the reasons why she was in this situation.

"You'll enjoy my family. I hope you aren't too worried about any of that," he said.

She was thankful for the conversation starter. "I'm excited to meet them. I'm sure everything will be fine. They know exactly what we are doing. They've been through it. So, it'll be nice being around two women who understand. And two people—well, four people including your brothers—who I don't have to completely pretend around. Living a double life might be hard." She interjected some humor into the situation, hoping to relieve some of the tension that radiated between them.

After the amazing kiss, she had been completely confused. She felt great tension from him; he had wanted to kiss her longer but he had finally broken away and she regretted it so bad. It felt like heaven, being in his arms. His kiss had been like nothing she had ever experienced in her life. She had wondered what a kiss from him with no restraints would be like, a kiss full of emotion and love. Or passion. She probably didn't need to think about passion too much. Because, to be honest, it would not take much for her to go there. She pulled her brain away from that thought.

"You looked beautiful today, in case I didn't tell you."

"Thank you. I know it was not real, but I loved that dress. It has been a whirlwind of a day between dress shopping, the ceremony, and now this flight. I'm exhausted."

"I feel bad, it was so rushed for you. You'll have to take some time for yourself and go to a spa for some pampering. Texas Hill Country is known for its very expansive spa region. I think there are spas hidden all over in that area. I'll make sure you, Allie, and Ginny have reservations for a day together. It will be a good way for you to get to know them. Okay?"

"I'm sure it will be lovely."

He looked out the window at the night that was passing by outside. "It's been awhile since I've spent any time at the ranch, to be honest."

She wanted so badly to go sit beside him. She

realized she really wanted to touch him but no, she wouldn't do that. Instead, she studied his expression. *Was he worried?*

"I'm sure you'll enjoy it. I know you'll be working some but don't you think getting back to your roots and relaxing some for the three months will be nice? That is your grandfather's demands, don't you think? I mean, when was the last time you took any time off?"

"It's been so long ago, I can't remember taking time off. I'm conflicted about it. I love my brothers and they love the land. But like I said, this hotel resort industry is busy and competitive and I love it."

"I have a question and don't get upset with me. But did you ever love the ranch? Your voice softens some when you mentioned it."

"I love the ranch. I loved being raised on a ranch and my roots run deep there. I even still wear my boots as often as I can. They fit with my lifestyle but, when I go to the ranch, at least when Granddaddy was alive, I always felt pressure. Maybe from him, maybe in my mind that I'm supposed to be there. But probably partly a rebellion on my part. I've always felt driven to make my own choice and, to be honest, if someone told me I need to do something, I don't take very kindly to it. Thus the reason it was very hard for me to go through with this marriage. But thank you for helping ease that situation for me."

"I'm glad I could be of service. This is going to be hard for both of us, in some ways, at some time. I'm sure we'll clash at points and, well, I hope that we can at least become friends or remain friends. I know I'm asking too much—I'm just your personal assistant."

"You're not only my personal assistant anymore. This marriage has taken us to another level. And there's no denying that. You'll never go back to *just* being my personal assistant." He looked at his watch. "Well, we still have about five hours. I think maybe we should try to get some sleep."

She was tired. They had waited until evening to fly out so that they could fly in the night and help with the long flight home. She had been too nervous to sleep. "That will probably be a good idea."

"There's a bedroom through that door there. You can sleep on the bed or, if you'd like, the chairs change into a bed also. But you'll be more comfortable in the bed."

"I don't feel right about taking the bed." She had never slept on a plane, especially in a bed on a plane. It was just foreign to her.

"Go on, your bags are in there. And if there's any turbulence or anything, you'll be notified. But go relax."

She realized that her bags had been stowed in that room; when they had boarded the plane, the chauffeur had carried them in there. "Okay, I honestly think it's going to take me all three months to get used to this luxurious lifestyle."

"There's anything you'd like to drink in there and snacks, too, if you get hungry. If you can't sleep, just relax. You'll be able to sleep tomorrow when your feet are firmly planted on land. Some people can't sleep on planes."

"Well, I normally don't. I'm normally working on my computer when I'm on an airplane, so this is a new experience for me. But I guess I will give it a go."

He chuckled. "I like the fact that you are willing to look at the bright side and experience new things. Have fun."

"I'm sure I will. With any luck, I'll close my eyes and be out in five seconds."

"That would be nice. Good night, Amber."

She walked to the door and looked over her shoulder. "Good night, Morgan." And then she went inside and closed the door behind her. The room was in the back of the plane and there was plenty of room for a bed against one wall. There was a small bar refrigerator on the other side; she went to it and pulled out a bottle of ginger ale. She didn't want anything with too much caffeine but she wanted something to give her a little bit of energy. She needed to go to sleep but she probably wouldn't be going to sleep. She went to the restroom and looked at herself in the mirror. "What are you doing?"

She gave herself one last warning look to keep a straight head during all of this. Then she went back into the bedroom, picked up her ginger ale, took a drink, and then climbed into the soft, very expensive sheets and covers on the bed. Despite thinking she wouldn't sleep, she did and she dreamed of Morgan…

* * *

She woke as the sun came through the windows of the bedroom. Amber sat up in bed with a start. *What time was it?* A glance at her watch let her know it was almost seven. They were supposed to land at seven-thirty. Amber jumped from bed and rushed to brush her teeth and freshen her makeup. She could not meet his family looking less than her best. The pressure was officially on.

As she walked into the cabin, he smiled from the kitchen area. "Good morning. I was just about to check on you. How about a cup of coffee?"

He was way too perky in the morning. "Perfect. I seem to be disoriented."

"Flying can do that to you. I put that in a paper cup with the lid on it since we'll be landing any minute now."

She took a seat and buckled her seat belt, since they would be landing soon.

He handed her a cup of coffee and then slid into the seat beside her. "I hope you slept well."

She inhaled the scent of coffee seeping through the opening of the lid, then took a sip and let it awaken her senses. *Better that than remember dreaming of the man's kisses last night.* "I did."

She sipped more coffee and then the pilot came over the sound system and told them they would land in five minutes.

"Did you?" she asked. He looked ridiculously non-wrinkled. *How did he do that?*

"I did. I'm about as comfortable on the plane as I am at home."

She shook her head. "That's actually a bit sad."

He laughed. "You think so?"

"Actually, I do. I think that means you have forgotten how life can be normal."

"Maybe. But I'm not complaining."

No, he wasn't, and she needed to remember that. The airstrip came into view below and within moments they were taxiing to a stop at the airstrip of the Rocking M. Four people waited beside an SUV.

She looked over at Morgan. "I'm assuming that's your brothers and Allie and Ginny."

"Yes, it is. They're eager to meet you. Ginny said she was eager to welcome you to the club. You'll find that Allie and Ginny are very different from each other but they're best friends. So, it's kind of worked out for them that both of them ended up falling for my brothers."

But it wouldn't work out for her, she reminded herself. "All right, well, I guess we're about to get this party started then."

He looked mildly entertained. "I'm just hoping by the end of the three months you are still thinking as positive as that."

"I think we're going to be okay. We have an understanding. Right?"

"Right."

By the time they climbed down the stairs, everyone stood next to the stairs, waiting for them.

Morgan had described his sisters-in-law and it wasn't hard to pick Ginny out of the bunch. She wore a bright-red beat-up straw cowboy hat with a large purple jewel in the center of it surrounded by some kind of small feathers. She had boots and jeans on and a shirt with fringe; she had her hand on her hip and studied Amber as she came down the stairs. Allie, on the other hand, looked about as sweet as honey, just as Morgan had described her, also wearing jeans and a pretty blouse.

Wade and Todd were both gorgeously handsome men. Morgan had not described them that way but they were just as handsome as he was and had a similar look, though with definite differences. Morgan had a more refined look, while Wade looked very much the cowboy in his hat and with his rugged jawline. Todd was leaner and had a wave to his hair that the others didn't.

Mr. J.D. obviously had produced three grandsons who looked very much alike in many ways and she had a feeling his son, their dad, looked very similar to them.

"Everyone, meet my bride, Amber," Morgan said as soon as they'd reached the bottom step.

Everyone welcomed her with smiles and hellos.

Ginny grinned. "Welcome to the club. I knew ole Morgan there would find himself a bride. And you look like you can hold your own."

Allie smiled. "We're really glad you're here. And we're going to help you get through this. Oh," she gasped. "Not that it's a terrible thing. What I meant was we're going to help you."

Wade put an arm around his wife and kissed her temple.

Ginny chuckled. "At times, these McCoy men can be hardheaded and we're going to help you get through in any way we can. Morgan says he thinks we need to go to a spa and I talked to Caroline yesterday—that's Morgan's cousin—she's going to join us. We're going to spend some of that McCoy money and take you to the best spa in the area. How does that sound?"

Morgan laughed. "I think you are probably giving my brother a run for his money, am I right?"

Todd grinned. "She is but I sure am enjoying watching her. I haven't smiled this much in my life. It's a good thing, Morgan. Maybe meeting the stipulations of Granddaddy's will be lucky for you too."

Morgan met her gaze, and his expression didn't tell Amber he felt that way at all.

They loaded into the SUV. Todd drove and Wade got in the passenger seat. Allie and Ginny climbed in the rear bench seat and left room for Morgan and Amber to sit in the middle. His brothers turned to look at Morgan and both grinned.

Todd spoke first. "Brother, we're glad you're home. I know, I know—you're not happy about Granddaddy's will but you haven't been home to stay at your house in so long, we're excited about having you here. I told Granddaddy thanks for the gift of bringing you home. I spoke to him the other day at the gravesite when Ginny and I took him some flowers."

"I'm against the idea of him forcing me home but I

149

haven't been here in so long. It took me a little while to get used to it, but we have a plan that will let me work while I'm here. With Amber being my assistant, she is going to help while we work from my home office. But I'm going to come check out the ranch and the vineyards while I'm here. More than just looking at it like I was visiting. I want to dig deep and take a look at the health of the company as a whole."

Wade rolled his eyes. "I knew you were going to say that." Wade looked at Amber. "He thinks he's the best businessman of the bunch. We have to break it to him gently over and over again that he's not. You get the picture—he thinks he's all that."

"I can feel the brotherly love." She laughed. They were pulling Morgan's strings and she could see he took it good-naturedly. She wondered whether they were always like this. But she did figure they were excited to see him here. She was so impressed with his granddaddy's ulterior motive to what he had done. She wasn't exactly sure what his long-term motive was, but if it was to get Morgan home full-time, he would fail. There was no way Morgan would give up the life he lived now.

CHAPTER TWELVE

For a man who didn't live on the ranch, he had built a beautiful home. It looked huge to her but there were homes bigger than this. But for a guy worth as much money as he was, it was probably considered a modest home. Still, it was beautiful, built with enormous stones and very rustic components. Beams rose high for the entrance and there were two stories, with massive windows. She was excited to find out what was inside. As they drove up the lane she glimpsed views of the river in the distance, it added to the beauty of the grounds and the beautiful pastures where cattle grazed all about, outside the fence surrounding the house.

She wondered how it would be living here with Morgan. She quickly reminded herself she wouldn't be here long.

She expected that everyone would get out but they didn't. Instead, Todd and Wade pulled their luggage from the rear of the vehicle and carried it to the front door. Allie and Ginny smiled from the backseat.

"We're not going to stay," Allie explained. "Y'all need time to settle in. We just wanted to welcome you to the ranch. We left our numbers in there with lunch, so just call one of us and we'll come running and set up our spa day."

"And don't let that dude get the better of you," Ginny warned. "There are rules and regulations to this arrangement. Stick to them. Be cautious with your heart. But you're a big girl, so good luck." She grinned. "Anyway, we're glad to have you aboard. Good luck with the hunk on this grand adventure you've entered into."

Amber almost laughed at Ginny's antics. In a very sarcastic way. She liked her a lot and Allie was the sweetest woman. She didn't know how Wade had found her but he had found a jewel, and Todd had found Ginny through Allie. She was eager to get to know all of them and really get to know their stories. She was intrigued, so intrigued by everything.

Ginny had reminded her that this was a grand adventure and that was how she would look at it from here on out. If she didn't, there was no telling what would happen if she let herself get too serious about any of this. Especially Morgan.

He held the door for her. "I assume we can forego me carrying you over the threshold."

She hesitated. "Yes. Save that for when you really get married again." She walked across the threshold, a little pain in her heart knowing that she would have really liked him to carry her over the threshold. But it was a slippery slope to heartbreak if she wished for things like that. It was better that he hadn't carried her over the threshold; he was the prudent one right now and she needed to be prudent also.

The entrance hall was beautiful, like something out of a magazine. The floors were polished to a high sheen and in large, irregular shapes with a goldish-yellow tone. It was amazing. "If the rest of this house is as beautiful as this floor, you have a very good eye, Mr. McCoy."

He laughed. "I had help from an interior designer but I love this floor. I didn't do it throughout because I thought it might be a little much. I usually come in through the garage. However, this is one of my favorite things about the house."

He led her into the great room. A staircase off to the right wound up to the second floor and a long area overlooked the beautiful living space. Huge round logs that had been hand polished or varnished were gorgeous; they shimmered up there in the skyline, they were so high up. It was massive, like a ski lodge. More huge windows overlooked the land and she could see the river, where the sun shimmered like spun gold.

"Again, beautiful."

"Kitchen is around the corner there. It's not part of the main area but it's got its own space that's open to this area." She followed him and yes, there was a kitchen. It was almost a chef's kitchen. Again, she wondered how often any of it had gotten used. On the massive bar sat a tray of what looked like fajita meat. And all the fixings for fajitas. Beside them was a pitcher of what she assumed was probably tea and a tray of vegetables and cookies.

"They left us a feast. We can warm it in the microwave. Easy fixings for later. Are you hungry?"

"Not yet. I would really like to see the rest of the house. And then maybe unpack."

"We'll go with that plan."

"Okay, let's do it."

He walked through the living space and down the hall, showing her where there was a game room, complete with a pool table. That would do her no good considering she didn't know how to play, but it looked great in the big rustic room with the vaulted ceilings. Beautiful Western oil paintings hung on the walls. *Western—was he a big Western fan?* This was a part of him that she did not know. The only Western thing that she knew about him was that he was from Texas and he wore cowboy boots sometimes. She had never seen him in jeans.

She walked to one of the paintings and saw the name of a famous Texas artist. "These are gorgeous."

"Thanks. I can't imagine having a talent like that." He smiled and turned in a circle, taking in the paintings that adorned the walls. There were five of them and all amazing.

Morgan was intriguing. Many men would have an elk or deer or something they hunted hanging on these walls but he was a hunter of beautiful art. *When would he have time to hunt, anyway?* And she didn't mind that about him.

"Yeah, I love this room. I've got paintings all throughout the house but that Thomas Moran there, of the Grand Canyon, is my favorite."

"I totally understand why."

They studied it for a moment, it was amazing, all of them were and she enjoyed viewing them and then they walked together up the stairs, and he carried her bags. He showed her to her room.

"Wait, no—this is your room," she said, looking at the obvious master bedroom suite. It also had huge windows out onto a second-floor balcony. "Wow, you really like big windows."

"I'm taking the smaller room across the hall. I've already had my things moved over there. I just want you to be comfortable while you're here. This is a great room and I do like big windows. I like letting the outside in."

He was being so accommodating to her. "I don't feel right about taking your space."

"Look, I'm hardly ever here. I basically only had a few pairs of pants and some shaving cream to be moved next door. Honestly, it's sad how little time I spend here."

She studied him. "It is sad. Why would you build this gorgeous place and not spend time in it?"

He shrugged and walked to the windows and stared out over the pastures that overlooked a river. "My history with wanting my independence and making my own way just made it kind of hard to come home."

She crossed her arms. "Why do I get the feeling that that's just an excuse?"

He cocked his head. "Why do you think that's an excuse?"

"Because you fly all over the world in that plane and unlike me, you hardly get jetlag, you're so used to it. You can get from Houston to here in, what? Thirty minutes? No, I don't believe that you just haven't come here because it's not convenient. You and your granddaddy didn't get along that well at all?"

"Look, it's not that simple. My granddaddy and I

clashed a lot. Not in a horrible way, but we just did better apart. We couldn't seem to ever be around each other without arguing. J.D. McCoy could be so obstinate."

She gave him a pointed stare. "And you aren't?"

"He didn't understand why I didn't just have that plane fly me in and out just like you suggested. He thought that this should be my main base and I shouldn't even have the apartment in Houston. But I got tired of always arguing with him about the same thing. If I lived here, I would have never had any peace."

"So, you don't like it here?"

"I do, but I'm not sure that I can live here full-time now. You are really full of questions."

"I guess if I'm married to you for three months, I want to know what makes you tick. I can't help myself."

"Right. I get it. But like I said, you're not going to really understand my and my granddad's relationship or why I don't come here."

"Are you afraid that if you come back here for an extended period of time, you might realize that you miss it and you want to be here more?"

He hesitated. "Maybe. You're very astute. And I think you're a troublemaker."

She laughed. "Maybe, but you're stuck with me for three months."

"And I have a feeling you're going to torture me as much as possible."

"Maybe. It might be fun. But seriously, I think coming home may be good for you. Your family is certainly happy about it."

He nodded thoughtfully. "They are, and I'm going to enjoy spending time with them. So there, are you happy?"

She laughed. "I am. Now, I think I'll let you leave and I'll enjoy this gigantic room you've given me."

He headed to the door. "I'll leave you to it then. And Amber..." He paused before closing the door. "I'm glad you're here."

She stared at the door long after he closed it. *He was glad she was here. And so was she.*

* * *

Morgan wondered whether his grandfather had ever

wondered if he had been part of the reason why Morgan didn't come home. Morgan wondered if, like Amber had suggested, that he had used his relationship with his grandfather as an excuse not to come home.

As he changed his shirt and pulled out a pair of jeans that he hadn't worn in a while, he couldn't help thinking about Amber and the fact that she made him think about things that he normally blocked from his thought process. And she had no problem doing it. It was another thing he wondered about. *Was that part of the reason he liked her as much as he did?* She challenged him on a regular basis and didn't seem to be bothered by the fact that she did challenge him. Oddly, the more he became successful, the more it seemed people didn't challenge him. Money seemed to do that. And, frankly, he had started to become bored with that. Even before the will, even before his grandfather died, he had become restless. Not that he would have told anyone. It was one of Morgan's major flaws that he didn't let anyone know what he was thinking.

Amber seemed to want to know what he was thinking and she prodded him more and more openly every day that he knew her, trying to find out what motivated him and what he was thinking. He had caught on to it. He grinned, thinking about it. Of course, he wanted to know more about her too; it was a natural curiosity considering they were now married. At least, he was telling himself that. But the reality was that even if they weren't married, he wanted to know more about Amber.

CHAPTER THIRTEEN

"I cannot believe that all three of my cousins are married." Caroline McCoy sat in one of the four chairs in the spa's relaxation room.

They all had green masks and cucumbers on their eyes. Caroline had picked them all up earlier that morning and driven them out into the Hill Country's tiny back roads that seemed to lead to nowhere until they came upon a fancy electric gate between two large white pillars.

Caroline had given a code; then the gate had opened and they had driven through and up a winding hillside to this stone and arched spa. It resembled something that she had seen in the Scottsdale area when she had been in Arizona, checking out one of the McCoy resorts. And it was a five-star rated experience. They had all had their massages and were now relaxing during their facials before they got their pedicures and manicures.

Amber had to admit she had always been so busy, this was one of the things she seldom did for herself. Very seldom, as in maybe she'd had two massages in her lifetime. And she never had a pedicure. Actually, it tickled her toes when someone worked on her feet but she was going to make it through this one without laughing. Manicures she did have every once in a while. So, this was a treat. Caroline obviously did this often.

"Well believe it, Caroline," Ginny drawled from beneath her green mask and cucumbers. "Because I love me some Todd McCoy and I'm never letting that hunk of good looking man go."

Caroline hooted with laughter and Amber laughed too and lifted a cucumber to peek at her new green masked friends.

"Ginny," Caroline said, grinning and making her

mask crinkle. "I love you, girlfriend. I love all of you. I am thrilled to have more women in the McCoy clan."

"I love Wade so much. He's my knight in shining armor and always will be. And now, Amber is here." Allie lifted her cucumber and caught Amber peeking. She smiled. "It's exciting." Then she lowered her cucumber and leaned back.

Ginny raised a cucumber as if realizing she was being watched and winked at Amber. "I think it was love at first sight." Then she snapped her cucumber back in place and chuckled.

Amber did the same, conflicted about what to say.

"I think it's wonderful that Amber fell for Morgan," Caroline said. "My older cousin can be a hard-nosed businessman, especially after Shannon. But everybody needs love and I am thrilled he's remarried and to you."

Amber felt like she was being watched and lifted a cucumber to find all three of them watching her. Amber took hers off, not able to have this conversation without her eyes wide open. They did the same.

"Thanks," she said. What else was she supposed to say?

"Maybe you can give him some balance. Hopefully he'll come home more often now. I mean Denton tours all over the place with his band and still makes it home to ground himself working his cattle. Morgan acts like he can't wait to leave the few times he does make it home."

Allie spoke up, "I haven't been around him, but just a few times, and not that I know very much, but I get this feeling that there was something between him and his granddaddy that kept him away. Wade says they were too much alike. But it would be nice to see him more often and you, Amber."

Amber was touched by the sincerity in Allie's words and expression.

Caroline frowned, making her green mask crinkle around the edges. "He needed somebody to love. And Amber I think you're perfect for him. But there was something between them. He has built a massive business and I don't think his granddaddy gave him enough credit for that. I think J.D. regretted their distance and disagreements. My granddaddy does, too."

Amber knew Caroline's grandfather was J.D.'s

brother. And both brothers had raised their grandchildren after their parents were all killed in a small plane crash. It was a terrible story but the grandfathers had both come through for their grandkids.

"Since we all lost our parents in the same accident, our granddaddies just kind of raised us together. We're very close. Morgan's almost like my older brother. Although he and Ash used to have knock-down drag-outs when they were growing up. They didn't always get along because they're both hardheaded. But we are all really close now—yeah, in a long-distance sort of way when it comes to Morgan and Denton and even Beck sometimes with his flying schedule. But everybody's always glad when we can get together."

Amber got the distinct impression—considering they were all telling her over and over again—that they wanted Morgan back in the fold. She liked Morgan the way he was. She would like Morgan however he was, but unlike them, she couldn't see him as a cowboy. He had been wearing jeans and boots since they were here but she still hadn't gotten used to it. Oh, he looked good, great actually, but she still hadn't gotten used to him out of his dress slacks and pressed dress shirts. Morgan being at the ranch all the time...didn't make complete sense to her despite the hard time she'd given him that first day back. She'd pressed him that day, just trying to feel him out on the situation.

Why she did that she wasn't completely sure but she couldn't seem to help it. There was an energy about him when he was working—fast-paced, he never slowed down and he was very intense. That intensity drew her. She was very attracted to it. But she was eager to see him out and about the ranch. She had a hunch it was good for him to be back on the ranch for a while.

She was looking forward to riding horses with him, seeing a side of him she'd never seen. They had decided that tomorrow they would ride horses or, depending on their workload, it might be the day after that. But she was very much excited about the fact.

"He's very intense and only certain people get around him at work." She toyed with the cucumber in her hand. *Should she say that he seemed like a man alone to her?*

"Oh, really?" Ginny asked. "Does he hold people

away from him?"

"Yes, I saw him from a distance. But until Mrs. Beasley, his personal assistant, had me come on the Hawaii trip, I hadn't really had a lot of or hardly any one-on-one interaction with him. I was just supposed to be on the trip to help out and then I went swimming and nearly drowned. He saved me. And that's how we met."

"He rescued you?" Caroline repeated, looking horrified. "I'm so sorry you nearly drowned. That's awful."

"Isn't it romantic?" Allie said.

"It's like it's meant to be," Ginny said, clearly delighted.

Caroline slapped her leg. "He literally saved your life. How much more romantic can it get? And then he asked you to marry him? It must have been love at first sight."

"Yes." Amber felt horrible about this. It was deception plain and simple.

"You didn't hesitate, did you?" Caroline's brows raised over knowing eyes.

"Well, no, I—"

"I think," Ginny drawled, winking again, "that it's very serendipitous that he was the one who rescued you. That love will always win."

Okay, that was very close to home. It was as if Ginny was reading her mind. "Yes, of course. But, I've been really a bit frazzled since nearly drowning and I love being at this spa. It was a great idea to come here. It has been a whirlwind since that day, so I've really enjoyed the girl time. And the insight into my boss's— husband's background."

Caroline grinned. "Well, girlfriend, I'll give you the lowdown on him anytime you want it. All you have to do is call one of us up and ask a question and we'll fill you in. I'm sure Ginny and Allie feel the same way, because we like you and are thrilled to have you as part of the family."

"We like you a lot." Allie smiled.

"Ditto." Ginny grinned.

Amber's heart clutched. "And I like all of you too. So very much." She could easily grow attached to this group who at the moment were her family. Something she hadn't had in so long. Not close family, anyway. She thought of her mom and dad and the horrible day they'd died in a car wreck when she'd been in seventh grade. Nothing had ever been the same since losing them. It felt good to belong but it would hurt all the more when the contract was up.

Morgan rode low and fast over the land that he'd pushed from his life. Wade and Todd rode beside him, flanking him on either side. Like they had growing up, they raced for the old oak tree at the far edge of this pasture. Their sure-footed stallions were competitive and they'd tossed coins for who rode which horse. He'd gotten Pepe Jack and the horse could fly.

He had forgotten this, this sense of freedom that came with the rush of the wind and the feel of the powerful animal churning up the ground beneath him as they charged across the wide-open land.

"Not today!" Wade whooped from just a foot behind him, his hat held high in his hand as he rode with the skill and ease of a man born to the land. He grinned as his horse sprang forward to take the lead.

Morgan laughed, and it felt good.

"Don't let him beat you," Todd hollered from half a

horse length behind him. He'd drawn the ride with less of a chance in this race and he knew it.

"Yah, Pepe, yah!" Morgan gave the horse more control and, just as he thought, Pepe didn't want to lose either. But he'd hesitated a moment too long and there was no catching Wade. His brother was laughing as he made it to the tree a step ahead of Morgan.

"You almost had me." Wade grinned.

"You faker. Nothing ever changes." Morgan hadn't remembered until it was too late that Wade always held a little extra back in a race.

"I knew this was probably my only shot at getting that over on you."

"I should have warned you." Todd laughed as he drew up next to them. "But Stampede and I, the slowest steed of all, were too busy trying to hang on by a hair."

Morgan gave him a curious stare. "You're a poet now?"

Todd grunted. "Hardly. That was just obvious."

"Not to me. Man, that was fun, fellas."

His brothers cocked their wrist over their saddle horns, relaxing, and grinned back at him as if he were an idiot.

Wade cocked his hat back and looked around. "Yeah, it's heck getting caught up in the big city and forgetting things like this."

"Home isn't a terrible place," Todd said. "There's more to enjoy than just flying in for the day for an event and flying back out. Granddaddy was right about you needing to come home for a while."

Morgan looked around and breathed in the crisp morning air, trying not to let the resentment at being forced home taint the joy he felt in this moment. "Yeah, I see your point. I've been away too long. How many times are y'all going to point that out to me?"

His brothers smiled. "Forever," they said in unison, as if reading each other's minds.

"Y'all still do it." Morgan laughed. It was something the two had done as little boys.

They all laughed, remembering.

Wade sobered first. "Granddaddy used to get a kick out of us doing that."

"Yeah, he did." Morgan's heart suddenly ached as the past nudged its way into his memory.

"I miss him," Todd said. "The place isn't the same

without him."

"Never will be." Wade sighed. "But man, were we blessed to know him, even if he was a strong-willed throwback who sometimes overstepped his boundaries."

"You're right." Todd took his hat off and slapped it on his thigh. "After Mom and Dad died, he and Grandma took us in and shoved their own grief to the back shelf to love on us, and give us everything in them. I miss Gram, too. Me and Ginny take flowers to their graves once a month. She started it—said he'd brought us together and she never knew him but she would always remember him because of the love he showed with his will."

Morgan frowned. "She said that?"

"Yeah, Ginny's not the hardnose she always seems to be. She's actually a big fluffy marshmallow stuck inside a small, feisty package."

"She's right, I think." Wade looked thoughtful. "Morgan, I hope you can find a way to make peace with him. I think, in his own way, that's what this is all about."

"I'm not saying we weren't blessed to have him and

Gram. We were, and I'm forever grateful for them. But at the same time, I'm not ready to roll over and be happy about what he's done. This forcing us to marry in order to keep what we all have poured our energy and dreams into isn't right. Okay, so that's just the way I see it and that's the way it will stay. Now, let's ride."

He barely squeezed a knee against Pepe and the horse loped forward as if more than ready to get back on track. Morgan knew he was. His brothers had their opinion and he had his. And he'd learned a long time ago that they all had minds of their own and that was okay.

They could thank J.D. for that too.

CHAPTER FOURTEEN

The afternoon was gorgeous and Amber could not believe how much she was loving her time here. She and Morgan had managed to make it through the first week fine. Both of them had been busy avoiding the attraction that sparked between them when their gazes met. They'd worked some and their horse riding had been put off until today. And so far, it had been good. At least she hadn't fallen off the horse, anyway.

Thank goodness, she didn't feel completely uncomfortable in the saddle. She had had a little riding experience—before her life had changed and she'd lost her parents. But that had been a long time ago. She was doing okay right now though, at least she was in the saddle still.

For the moment anyway.

"What is that?" She halted the very gentle horse Morgan had put her on. It helped her ride with as much dignity as she could muster after such a long time.

Morgan had ridden ahead of her to check out something he saw near a bush, thinking maybe it was a baby calf. She had been caught up admiring him as he galloped away from her, tall in his saddle and with the ease of a cowboy who'd been raised riding. And he had been. This was where he started, a cowboy working on the ranch. Not a debonair CEO of a billion-dollar resort conglomerate.

"It's a dog." He stepped from the stirrup to the ground.

"*What?* Way out here alone?" She started to dismount.

Morgan held up a hand. "Wait, let me make sure it's safe. She's not looking exactly happy to see us. I'm wondering if she's hurt or dehydrated."

He eased toward the bush. Then he halted and looked back over his shoulder at her. "She has four puppies. And she isn't looking so good."

"Oh, no, poor girl." Amber was already climbing down from the horse's back despite him telling her not to. She hurried over to kneel beside him. A medium-sized dog peered at them with weary eyes. It was shaggy and dirty and nestled against her were four puppies, nursing. The mama's tail flopped in a welcome. "I don't think she's dangerous. But I believe she needs help."

"I think you're right." He held his hand out for the mom to sniff. When she licked his hand, Morgan looked over at Amber. "I think we have a friend. I'm going to try to pick her up. Do you think you can carry the puppies? I'll see if I can get her in the saddle with me."

"I figure I can manage four puppies if you can manage her. She's big."

"I've carried calves in the saddle with me bigger than her."

Amber gaped at him in disbelief. "I cannot get into my head that you were once a working cowboy."

He laughed. "In the flesh. My granddaddy worked us like he worked all his hired help. He had us up at sunup and most summer nights we didn't come inside until after sundown. I've wrangled cows, branded calves, and baled hay with the best of them. I promise you, I'm not just a pretty face." He winked at her then walked past with the listless mama dog.

"Whew, ya got that right," Amber muttered to herself, watching him walk away. "And you rescue dogs too," she called after him, feeling a new measure of respect for the man she'd only just begun to start getting to know. Then she gasped and spun to the whimpering puppies. "I am so sorry, little doggies. Come here. Let's get you home." She had on a tank top under her blouse and so she stripped off her cotton button-up and gently laid the babies inside. Then, gathering it in her arms, she strode toward her horse. She admired the way Morgan's jeans stretched across his—okay, she was not admiring his butt.

Her cheeks flaming, she walked past him just as he settled into the saddle with the dog in front of him.

"Why are you so red?" He studied her face and his eyes dropped to her arms where she had the puppies cuddled in them.

"Because...it's hot out here."

His gaze met hers. "Yeah, you're right about that. Let's get this family some help. I think she needs to see a doctor fast. We'll take them straight to the vet when we get back to the house."

Amber was pleased that Morgan hadn't even hesitated about the dogs. She managed to climb into the saddle with one arm while cuddling the shirt full of puppies with the other arm. "I'm ready. I'll follow you."

"You might turn into a cowgirl yourself," Morgan said, as he rode past her. "Well done."

She swallowed hard, feeling an unbelievable sense of happiness fill her at his compliment. "Thanks. You too."

As soon as they arrived back at the house, Morgan placed the mother dog in the backseat of his truck. Amber carefully laid the babies in the seat beside her as he went into the house to get a few towels to make a bed. He strode back outside to find her petting the mother and talking to her, trying to make the dog comfortable with her voice and the soothing feel of her hands. He had brought a bowl of water and a little bit of meat from the refrigerator considering he didn't have any dog food. He set the bowl in the seat beside the mother and she immediately drank from it, looking very grateful to have it. Then he held his palm out with pieces of brisket.

"You said we were going to take her to your cousin, the vet?"

He had told her on the ride in that his cousin, Caroline's brother Ash, was the veterinarian in town and he would take the dogs there to be checked out. "Yes, so as soon as she has eaten a little bit more of this meat and drank some more of that water, we'll get on the road. She's acting like she's not in terrible shape but she might be dehydrated. We might have gotten to her soon enough, although I'm not sure why her leg is hurting her. He'll have to tell us that."

Moments later, they were driving into town. Stonewall wasn't a big place. And Ash had placed his clinic in a central location to all the ranches, so he wasn't actually in any of the towns in their area. Instead, he was out in the country, a short drive from Stonewall on a plot of land belonging to the McCoy

Ranch belonging to Talbert.

When they arrived, Lynette, Ash's office manager, hurried from behind the counter. Morgan had called ahead and told them he was bringing the mother and puppies that were in bad shape. Lynette was a firecracker, about sixty-five years old, and loved animals and people. She had a whole house full of animals, along with a bunch of grandkids.

She gave him the once-over. "Morgan McCoy, it is so good to see you. Now, let's see what you've got. Oh, isn't she a poor dear."

"She is, Lynette. And it's good to see you too. Amber, my…wife, has an armload of babies."

Lynette gasped, "You got married? What has come over you boys? Your granddaddy would be so over the moon about this. Does Talbert know? Oh, I'm sorry, Amber. It is so very wonderful to meet you." She looked at Amber with total disbelief then smiled. "This is just marvelous. I can't believe we didn't know you were getting married. Anyway, come on back and let's take care of these sweeties you two have rescued."

He followed her down a hall into a patient room and he gently laid the dog on the examination table. "It's okay." He gently rubbed her neck as Amber set the puppies beside her in the shirt. They immediately snuggled close to their mom; she lifted her head and tried to look at them but didn't seem to have the strength.

Amber looked alarmed. "I'm worried."

Morgan couldn't help himself; he rubbed her arm. "Ash will take good care of her."

She nodded but didn't look convinced.

"He will," Lynette assured her. "He's a mighty fine veterinarian. We are proud he shot for his dreams and came back here to open up this practice. There's not a better animal doctor in the state of Texas, I can assure you."

That seemed to lift some of the worry from Amber's eyes and he was glad.

"I hope he can help them."

"You are a sweetie. And Morgan's wife. I am so thrilled. I always knew this boy would settle down with a sweet woman who loved animals. Your husband used to rescue animals. I worked for Doc Mason before he retired and Morgan was always bringing in all kinds of animals."

"Really?" Amber looked at him. "I learn something

new about you every day."

"I guess I did do that." He hadn't thought about that in a very long time. "Where is Ash?"

Lynette waved toward the door. "He'll be here in just a minute. He's out back—he had a calf he had to pull."

"I'll head out there. Maybe I can hurry him up."

Lynette placed her hands on the mother dog and stroked her gently, taking his place as he headed outside.

He looked at Amber. "I'll be right back. Will you be okay?" He had been so impressed with Amber in how she'd helped rescue the dog and puppies. She just jumped in and was all for stopping her afternoon plans to make sure these animals got help.

She looked at him with eyes that melted into him. "I'm fine. Help your cousin so he can come help us."

Not thinking about what he was doing but compelled to comfort her, he bent and placed a quick kiss to her forehead. "I'll be back."

It was only after the door closed behind him that he realized how naturally the act of affection had come to him.

CHAPTER FIFTEEN

Ash strode into the room and Amber knew instantly that he was Morgan's cousin. They had features that were distinctive: the strong jawline, the dark eyes, the dark hair, and there was a masculinity to him that she had grown used to when she looked at Morgan. She knew he was Caroline's brother and she knew all of her brothers were single. He was as handsome as Morgan, but she felt not one ounce of attraction to him other than noticing he was handsome. No, she was very attracted to Morgan. And the fact that he had been so kind to this dog only made her more attracted to him.

"Hi." He smiled at Amber before focusing on the dog. He took her face into his hands and looked into her eyes, then her ears and then her mouth. Then he ran his hands along the dog's body, through all her matted hair; when he touched her left leg, the dog jerked. "Sorry, little lady," he said gently.

Amber kept near the puppies to make sure they didn't fall off the exam table. She liked his gentle way and looked at Morgan and found him looking at her. He'd kissed her forehead earlier and her skin still felt wonderfully warm where his lips had been. "He's good," she mouthed.

"Told you so," he mouthed back, holding her gaze and sending her heart racing.

She inhaled and tried to keep her hopes and dreams under control. *She could love this man if she let this infatuation get out of hand.*

"I think she might have injured her hip, maybe jumping out of something. I'm not sure if she got hit by anything but it appears to just be sore. So that's good. The rest of the issue is she appears to be dehydrated. She didn't have any food and she's given birth to these babies, so I think when we get some fluids and food in them, and get them some shots to take care of them, in a couple of days, you'll have yourself what looks like a very nice Golden Retriever mix. And puppies. Are you all up to taking care of them?"

Amber waited, not sure what to say.

"We're up to it. It's been awhile since I've had a dog but I remember how to take care of one. You just give her whatever she needs and then we will come back to pick her up as soon as you say it's okay. And let me know what I need to pick up—we'll go ahead and get it and have it ready for her. It angers me when people throw dogs out—I think that's probably what happened, don't you?"

Ash nodded. "It's sad and it happens a lot. Or she could've run off. Sometimes when a dog is pregnant, they run off. It might be a good idea to put up some pictures of her and just see if someone's missing a pregnant dog. I didn't feel a chip in her ear or anything, so she hasn't been chipped. No tags but it's still a possibility that she has owners. Just look at her—she's too sweet, too calm, too nice. If you want to take a picture of her with your phone right there, I'll have them printed off and we'll put one up in here at the office. Maybe you can send some of them out to the local friends and businesses and just kind of get the word out. They have lost dog forums online, too. You might want to try that. It's not unheard of to have a dog like this and someone's looking for it—someone's lost it, so you might very well not end up with a dog."

"Well, I hope that if someone is missing her that they find her picture and can be reunited." Amber hated the idea of someone who wanted the dog or loved the dog missing her. If she had a dog, she would hate if something had happened to her. "Thank you for looking after her so much. And it was nice meeting you. Your cousin's a good guy. I've always liked working for him."

Ash studied her. "Well, I hope you enjoy being married to him more than you enjoy working for him. That is pretty cool that y'all have a good working relationship. Me, I don't think Lynette would want to marry me. I've asked her several times but she won't take me up on it and her husband, Harvey, won't like it too much either, so I'm just stuck here—a lonesome bachelor, all by myself. Although my granddad has been acting a little bit suspicious lately. And I'm not sure what's up. But he's been watching your brothers and now you get married…I have a sinking suspicion that he's getting ideas. I hope not. I figure I'll get married when I get married and I don't want my granddaddy pushing me. Or Penny. I can tell with the wedding receptions that Penny threw for Wade and then for Todd that she's kind of enjoying herself too. Speaking of which, when are y'all having one?"

Amber knew Penny was an old friend of his granddaddy's who had called to set up a reception but Morgan hadn't given her an answer yet.

"Penny called but I haven't given her a date." He looked at her. "I guess we better decide on the date. If we don't figure one out, she's going to do it anyway. So probably in a couple of weeks."

"Any date you want is good with me." *A party.* There would be dancing and they would pretend to be happily married. *And she would be in his arms again.* The thought sent a shiver of anticipation through her. "Ash, please take good care of this little family and I'll do whatever you need me to."

"You're great. I know when I release them they'll

be in good hands."

After they left the veterinary clinic, they drove to the feed store and picked out a dog bed and the food that Ash had recommended. It was the first time they'd been out and about together and obviously word had spread that Morgan had married. Everybody was curious about the woman who had stolen Morgan McCoy's heart. She was touched, and she and Morgan just went along with everybody's curiosity. For the first time since they had started this marriage, she began to feel a little bit deceptive. But both Allie and Ginny had told her that she would have those feelings. They'd said it was hard but that it couldn't be helped and came with the territory. Amber hadn't realized how deceptive it would feel, though.

She at least could console herself with the fact that she really was crazy about him. And the more she was around him, the more she knew that she could seriously fall for him. She just needed to start figuring out how to get him to stop being so set on her leaving at the end of this three-month period. But she had no idea how to get him to see her as a forever kind of wife instead of a temporary wife.

She needed not to get ahead of herself. She told herself that as they arrived back home and entered the kitchen. He held the door open for her and she brushed by him. Her skin tingled when he grabbed her arm as he closed the door and she paused to look at him.

"That was a day, wasn't it?" His hand lingered on her arm as tingling sensations buzzed through her. "You were a real trooper out there." His gaze held hers.

Her heart pounded and she fought the urge to move closer to him. "You were great, too." She told herself to relax. "I enjoyed spending the day with you."

"I enjoyed spending the day with you. You were very good with the dogs."

"You were too. So, you used to save animals and you had a dog?"

He pulled his hand away from her arm and she wished he would put it back. He moved into the kitchen and she followed.

"I did have a dog. I really loved that dog. You want me to make some coffee?"

"I would love some coffee." She took a seat at the bar, putting a barrier between them so she wasn't tempted to go hover next to him. She watched him move around the kitchen. She didn't think she would ever get tired of watching him. He moved with an agility and grace that was both masculine and sexy. *Who was she kidding—the man was just sexy.*

Morgan knew he needed to go check his email or clean his room or something, anything other than have coffee right now with Amber. After saving the mama dog and puppies and seeing Amber completely devoted to the rescue, he was not in his right mind. As much as he was trying, he could not get that picture of her out of his mind: holding those puppies in her arms, wrapped in her shirt and cuddling them so close and looking up at him with those gorgeous eyes.

He filled two mugs with coffee then turned to find her watching him. His heart felt light as he held the mug out to her. "Let's take this out to the porch."

"Lead the way and I'll follow." She took it, her fingers brushing his and sending heat through him.

He held the door for her then led the way past the couches and chairs and headed to the far end of the large patio to the old-fashioned porch swing. He should have stopped at the chairs but he didn't want to. He might regret it but tonight he wanted her to sit with him on the swing. He sat down and placed his coffee mug on the side table. Then he patted the seat beside him. "Swing with me?"

She took a deep breath and nodded, looking as nervous as he felt. She eased down, clutching her coffee mug with both hands. She sat stiffly and sipped her coffee.

"You were really good today."

She looked over at him. "You were pretty incredible yourself, cowboy."

He chuckled. "Cowboy, huh?"

"You were impressive today."

"You were impressive yourself. We…made a good team today."

She bit her lip and her eyes mellowed, and all he could think about was kissing her again. He had forced himself not to think about the way she'd responded to his kiss at the wedding. Now it was blocking all other thoughts.

"Morgan," she whispered. "W-what are you

thinking about?"

She had a troubled expression. And her eyes were worried. "Nothing in particular. Why do you look so worried?"

"Because you were very intensely in thought and I don't believe you."

"Don't believe what?"

"I don't believe that you're telling me the truth. I believe you had something very troubling on your mind. You, Morgan McCoy, don't like to talk about things that trouble you. You're a problem solver—you fix things. And when you're troubled, you think deeply about it. Like just now."

He couldn't get anything past this woman. How could she read him so well? It was as though from the very moment he rescued her, she was connected to him on some other level. Some level no one had ever been connected to him on. "I'm not sure how to answer what you just said."

"That's because you're not used to people pressing you. I've said that before. You're used to giving people an answer and them going on. I'm curious, do your brothers not push for real answers?"

"My brothers know me. They know when to not push, unlike someone on this porch."

"Just chalk it up to the fact that I don't know you very well. It's why I push."

"Actually, as disturbing as it is, I'm beginning to think you know me better than a lot of people."

They stared at each other, holding each other's gaze as the dusk crept down upon them. Her lips curled slowly upward. "Maybe it's because you saved me, because you rescued me and I know I would be dead...if it weren't for you, I wouldn't be here right now."

"You don't have to be always grateful to me for that." It bothered him more and more every time she thanked him for saving her and reminded him that she wouldn't be here without him.

She set her mug on the table on her side of the swing and turned back to face him. "But I do feel that way. And I look at you and I want to know more. I know, I know—we're going our separate ways but I can't lie about it. I want to know what makes you tick and what you're thinking and what's bothering you. And I'm going to push because I have a gut instinct that maybe you need me to push."

He didn't like the way this was going. "I don't need you…to push," he clarified. He couldn't honestly say he didn't need her, because, at the moment, looking at her, he had a big need. He wanted more than ever, or *needed* to pull her into his arms and kiss her. He wanted to or needed to see whether she felt as good in his arms as the day they had married and he'd kissed her. Only this time, he wanted to kiss her, kiss her long and deep and slow, and wanted her to kiss him back. He needed it—though he denied it. Maybe it was just a want but whatever it was, she was driving him crazy. And normally, if someone pushed, he pushed them away. But right now, the way she pushed him only had him wanting to get closer to her. It was a really weird place for him to be in.

"You're doing it again—thinking deeply, troubled. What are you thinking?"

Unable to sit there any longer, he stood. "What if I don't want to tell you what I'm thinking? I'm not accustomed to answering to people." He bit the words out, irritated now that he was even considering answering her question. He wasn't used to answering people's questions. People answered his questions;

people did what he wanted—people who worked for him, especially. But that was the dilemma: she worked for him but she was also his wife, however temporary it might be. He raked his hands through his hair. "I didn't mean to snap at you."

She stood. "It's okay." She walked over to the edge of the porch, put her hands on the railing, and studied the river in the distance. "You know," she said when he didn't answer her or say anything else—he was too busy looking at her, "I don't have a right to ask you those questions but I already told you why I do it." She turned to look at him, her back leaning against the railing and her hands behind her.

He stepped toward her, unable to stop himself. "You want to know what I'm so deep in thought about?" He lifted a strand of her hair from her shoulder and rubbed the silky strand between his fingertips. "I'm trying to talk myself out of wanting to kiss you."

"Oh." The word was barely audible as it escaped from her lips.

He stepped closer. "Yeah, you asked and there it is. You're driving me crazy." He leaned forward and hesitated just before his lips met hers. "I think about this all the time," he murmured.

"Me too," she whispered. "But...Morgan, I can't help wanting more than what we agreed on. I want to get to know you better. I have to confess that I love being around your family. Your sisters-in-law are marvelous and Caroline is so funny, we have such a good time together. And so many people really believe we married for love. Even Caroline believes that you married me because we fell in love after you saved me. I know it's ridiculous, but honestly—I shouldn't say this because it's going to be out of place—but I wish that maybe you had fallen in love with me."

Her words stunned him. His gut tightened and he cupped her cheek. He had the oddest longing for it to be true himself. *What was happening?* "Why do you think or want that?"

"Well, you're handsome—yes, I admit that. But I like your intensity. I like your dedication. And yes, maybe that was trivial but even though I never met you, I saw the intensity when you worked. And the dedication that you had—I admire that. But I also saw you with Mrs. Beasley. You never treated her badly; you were kind to her. You were always respectful to women. In this day and age, that is huge. Maybe that's why I had such a crush. I've worked in offices where that wasn't so. And then knowing you'd lost your wife made me want you to be happy again. It's not until after you saved me and I started being around you that I knew just how great a man you are. Then, today, you were so kind to that dog and, well, I think my crush solidified a little bit more. You're a good guy, Morgan."

"And how do you feel about my actions right now?" he asked, not letting thoughts of Shannon taint the moment.

"I can't help thinking that we're not in an office anymore. And I would love it if you kissed me again."

* * *

Amber couldn't believe that she had just asked him to kiss her. But, as she had decided, she had one shot at this and she wanted to make the most of it. And now, as he stared into her eyes her pulse went crazy and her knees went weak.

And then he lowered his head and kissed her. His arms went around her and he pulled her close. She was lost in a whirlwind of emotions that took her breath away just as much as the feel of his lips against hers did. She was in trouble and there was no way she could deny it.

When he finally pulled back, she was breathless and jittery and completely out of her element. *Who was she, anyway? What was she thinking?* Morgan was far more experienced than anyone she had ever kissed before. She might have just stepped off a cliff because she could be in great danger of having bitten off more than she could handle. She stared into his eyes and she knew he could probably see straight through her. She felt childish and vulnerable and wondered what he was thinking. He stared at her, unblinking, as if he might be stunned too.

"I think we may be treading in areas that neither of us need to go," he said slowly but he didn't back away. He continued to hold her loosely, as if he didn't want to let her go.

But she knew he would. She could read it in his eyes. And why she thought she knew him so well, she didn't know...because she didn't. But she took a deep breath. "I'm not afraid." *Why had she said that, she wanted to know.* Afraid? She was shaking in her boots—if she had boots on. She had been alone for so long. She realized that it would be really wonderful to be attached to this family that he seemed so careless to cherish. She wondered why he built this house and didn't come here to stay.

"I'm not one to toy with, Amber. I can tell you that I'm over-the-top attracted to you. You will make some man a wonderful wife one day. He'll be proud of you—proud of all the things that you do and are capable of. And you'll have a wonderful family. I have no doubt you'll succeed at whatever you want. But right now, right here, I don't know what else to offer you. But I won't let this marriage go on after three months."

He was warning her. He was warning her to back off. Warning her that they could move forward—they could explore this marriage but he was warning her that there would be nothing more. And that was the kind of man he was; it was what she had been trying to tell him before. That was why she had this crazy crush on him that she knew now was more.

She straightened, stepped to the side and he let her go. "I think it's time for me to go to bed. Good night, Morgan." Then she turned and headed inside, telling herself to heed his warning.

But she didn't think she could.

CHAPTER SIXTEEN

He didn't sleep well and when he woke, he wasn't in any kind of mood for anything. He climbed out of bed early, left the house, and drove to the stables. *How long had it been since he had an early morning ride?* Something he used to do when he was growing up. When he was frustrated, riding always helped. He couldn't recall the last time he'd done it; he couldn't recall the last time he was actually aggravated enough to ride a horse.

Business was business; he very seldom lost his temper or got disgruntled in business. He was very diplomatic in his business dealings. He didn't let emotions get to him. He could let any resort go that he was trying to bid on. But once he had the resort in his portfolio, it became part of the McCoy franchise and he didn't let it go. But when someone in business let their emotions dictate how they bought or sold property, it was their downfall and he didn't do that.

This was different. This was not business; this was again his grandfather. Granddaddy had put him in a situation and he didn't like it. He had wanted more than anything to continue kissing and getting to know his wife better last night.

He wanted to open up to her; he wanted to get her to open up to him. He wanted to know about her background. He wanted to know everything there was about Amber and that was a place he had never been to before, not even with Shannon. With Shannon he now knew it had been more shallow and not love. Now, more than his hormones were involved, his emotions were deeply involved but she would get hurt and he wouldn't do that. So he let her walk away and he smiled or let his thoughts convey goodwill to her. He was not calm on the inside as she walked away, not all through the night nor this morning.

The stables were dimly lit—cowboys started early but not many of them started at five a.m. He would see the sunrise this morning. He had the big black gelding out of the stall and saddled within just a few minutes. As the rooster crowed somewhere in the distance, he rode out from the stable toward the open land. And it felt good.

One more reminder of things he had let go, things he had not let draw him back here to this land. He had his granddaddy to thank for that, too. But he wasn't thinking about his granddaddy; he was thinking about Amber. And what he was going to do to make it through all the weeks that stretched out before them. *He was not going to kiss her again.*

After he had ridden awhile, he stopped on a hill, his arm resting on the saddle horn, to watch the sunrise on the horizon. The morning woke with a pink tinge of sun, laying the soft blue and pink morning light across the pastures to wake the cattle dotting the land; they moved slowly as they began to stir. He had missed this. *He wouldn't stay away as long now.* That knowledge stung and his gut twisted.

He had loved his granddaddy but their

stubbornness, their determination to both be right had dug a hole between them that couldn't be crossed. As he sat there watching the sun rise, grief that he hadn't let fully embrace him cut a hole through him. Regret, anger, and remorse tangled together. He hung his head and let himself feel it for the first time in all these months since his granddaddy was buried.

What a waste the last years had been between them.

* * *

They picked the dog up two days after the kiss that still hung between them like an elephant. The puppies were adorable. They all had seemed to grow just in the couple of days they were gone and Amber lost a little bit of her heart just watching them squirm in the backseat as they nestled against their mother. Ash had said they had done well and the mother was going to be fine. Her leg was already feeling better and he felt like soon she would be walking around without a limp.

No word had come in on anyone looking for a missing dog and she had hoped that if someone was looking for Goldie, as she was calling the golden-red dog, that they would show up soon. If they didn't, she would be in trouble, having lost her heart by the time they'd gotten home.

She and Morgan were being very careful with each other. Today, he hadn't been at home when she woke up. She was in the kitchen when he walked in, looking a little bit wild, as if he had ridden across the pastures and run his hands through his hair several times. She couldn't help but wonder whether he hadn't slept. But that would be wishful thinking on her part that he might have stayed up, thinking about kissing her again.

Goodness, how old was she anyway? They were adults and this was ridiculous, especially when she admitted that she had stayed awake most of the night thinking about that kiss and repeatedly admonishing herself for having pushed for something that probably would never happen.

"I've got a bed ready for them in the utility room. I mean, we're not going to put them outside yet, are we?" she said when they arrived home with the dogs.

"No, they're not going outside. These puppies need to get their strength up and she doesn't need to be outside. They're not inside dogs; they need to run and

Hope Moore

romp but while they're here, they'll be comfortable. If no one comes and claims Goldie, as you're calling her, then we'll have to find her a home. As much as I like her, I'm not here enough. But maybe Wade and Allie would want a dog. I'd like to see her when I do come home."

"And I want to know that she's got a good place. Allie and Wade would be wonderful, so that's what I'll be hoping for. I'll want to know how she's doing and I can call and check on her if they agree to take her. We'll talk them into it."

She didn't believe that Allie would turn these puppies away; she knew that Allie would fall in love with them just like she had. She held two of them cuddled up against her and he placed the other two in her arms, then lifted Goldie from the truck and set her gently on the ground so she could test her leg and then walk beside them. She thought probably that he, too, would be glad to know where they were.

"We'll pile up on them. They'll take her—I'm sure they will. She's a sweet dog."

"Thank you. Now let's get them settled." She walked into the house and he walked slowly beside the

206

dog, following her. They settled the puppies in their basket that she had readied for them. It was a big, comfortable bed that they had picked up at the feed store. She was happy to watch as Goldie curled up on the bed and then her puppies snuggled with her.

She looked up at Morgan. "I'm so glad we went horse riding that day. I hate to think about what would've happened if we hadn't found them. I don't think they would've made it. It's a wonder what some fluids being pumped into her and food have done but with the heat and lack of moisture, she wouldn't have made it."

"Nope, she wouldn't have, so we had just the right timing, didn't we."

The way he said it eased the tension between them. "Yes, we did. We did good."

He smiled. Butterflies jostled around in her stomach, which was not good. She needed to not do that; she needed to get those butterflies wrangled into submission and back into their cage because, well, she was on a one-way trip to a broken heart if she continued this nonsense.

"I think I'm going to call Allie and Ginny and see if

they want to go to lunch and help me buy those clothes I need to buy. I'm just about out. I washed clothes again yesterday but I'm kind of tired of wearing the same thing over and over again."

"I think that's a great idea. I need to make some phone calls anyway and I'll probably go over and see Todd. He wanted to show me a few things at the vineyard and ask my advice."

"Then I guess we have a plan. Okay, I'm going to go make my calls. Talk to you later." She turned and headed back up the stairs into her room, where she picked up her phone. She quickly called Allie and they made plans to meet and go shopping that afternoon. She needed to go shopping every day; she needed to find something to keep herself away from Morgan.

At least until she could get these crazy emotions she was feeling under control. Either that or she was just going to drive the man crazy and he was going to divorce her and lose everything. She couldn't let that happen. She felt too much of a heavy responsibility for that. It was ridiculous. But she could handle it, especially with her new friends. They would support her. And she could talk to them. That was the reason she didn't call Caroline. What was Caroline going to think when she found out the truth? She hated to think about it. Caroline was a pistol and she would probably never let her live it down. Either that or she might hurt Morgan when she found out the truth. Either way, she couldn't talk to her right now, so hanging out with Allie and Ginny was the best.

* * *

Morgan stared at his brother as they walked through the vineyards. He hadn't been to the vineyard since he'd come for the festival a month ago. As kids, they had run through these vines, playing chase, similar to how some kids used cornfields to play hide-and-seek in. If they hadn't been running through the vineyard, they had been riding through the pastures at the ranch. Granddaddy had made certain that they had a great childhood; despite losing their parents, they had been raised in a great environment. And Morgan knew his granddaddy loved him and in his own way he loved his granddaddy. But they just hadn't seen eye to eye in business.

"You're doing a great job, Todd. Why do you need my advice on anything?"

Todd put his hands on his hips and leveled his gaze on him. "I'm not asking for your advice. I'm actually wanting to give you some advice. I want to tell you to let it go."

Morgan frowned. "Let what go?"

"The aggravation, anger, regret—everything you have inside you that's been boiling up between you and Granddaddy all these years. Let it go. Granddaddy was a great guy. You know that he raised us, running through these fields and with the freedom to ride through the pastures, to become the men that we are today. He had his own way and he tried to steer us in the way he wanted us to go. But I've come to realize just how much he loved us and as weird as his will is, it was his last way to reach out and try to give us one last shot at what he thought would make us happy. And, Morgan, he was right. And I don't know if you can agree with that because you two had more of a contentious relationship but I can tell you just from having Ginny in my life that I'm very grateful to Granddaddy for giving me this shot at finding happiness."

Morgan just stared at his brother. *Why did everybody think he needed to talk about his granddaddy? That he was holding a grudge against his granddaddy?* He could feel it even in Amber, that she thought there was something he needed to make peace with. Maybe they hadn't come right out and say it but he could feel it.

"Look, Todd, you know I kind of envied Wade that he and Granddaddy were so much alike that they actually connected like they did. Wade's more laid-back—knew what he wanted. Out of all of us, he was most content, and yet he was busy and hadn't found a wife yet. And then Granddaddy went and did what he did. If Wade hadn't found Allie, he would have lost all that he worked for. I don't find that as a good thing that Granddaddy did. Yeah, I'm glad that you and Wade are happy and that you found the loves of your lives but do I think Granddaddy was being kind when he did it or that he was doing the right thing? No—no way. He was controlling us one last time. It just happened to work out for y'all.

"So forgive me if I don't totally agree with

everything you're saying. Yeah, I am aggravated at Granddaddy still deep down, but I don't want to sit on the couch and talk about it. I'm getting over it. And Amber and I are doing fine. Our agreement is going to work out, so no thanks to Granddaddy, I'm going to get to keep what I've worked so hard for and what he worked for. I don't get it. I don't get what he did. And I also don't want to keep having this conversation."

Todd raked a hand through his hair then slapped his beat-up straw hat against his thigh. "I'm not going to keep bringing it up. I just felt like I needed to speak my mind. Amber's great. I'm glad y'all are getting along and in the end, I hope it works out for y'all. However y'all want it to work out—be it you go your separate ways or not—I just thought I needed to let you know how I felt since I was as mad as you are—or almost—when it came my turn to do this. I just want you to relax and be glad you're here and enjoy your time here. And I do want to ask your advice on some things."

"What?"

"I'm thinking of expanding the vineyard into a guest inn—a resort of sorts. And I'd like your thoughts on that since that's your expertise. Wade and I and

Ginny and Allie have discussed it a little bit. We have this beautiful place out here that we've grown and have gotten to enjoy all our lives—well, Ginny and Allie are starting to enjoy—and we're going to all have kids one day. And well, we were all just sitting around the fire pit one evening, discussing it, and we thought we'd ask you."

Morgan was shocked, to say the least. "A resort? You mean, more of like a bed-and-breakfast on a bigger scale—a few rooms? Not like a resort or hotel, because I don't think that's a good idea at all. Think about all the land it would take. It would take the charm away."

"Yeah, a bed-and-breakfast would be cool. Maybe a villa—ten rooms maybe?"

"We're talking like honeymoon suites or weekend getaways or kids? Because for what you're talking about, you're going to have to make some decisions. Getaway weekenders who are single aren't going to want to spend their time listening to kids being rambunctious and jumping around next door. I'm not saying I have anything against kids or they have anything against kids, but I'm just saying that it would be a choice. In a small space like that, I think."

"But you're thinking it would be possible and a good idea?"

Morgan took a deep breath and turned as he surveyed the vast property. The vineyard was six acres; they had more in another area. They had plenty. But this area was big enough to harvest a large amount of grapes while also feeling cozy. "Where are you thinking about doing it?"

"We thought about doing it near the river access. It would be an added visual—they could see the river from the deck in the back and the vineyards from the front. We could build the building so that there were private balconies and they could choose which view they wanted. We thought about doing it on the vineyard and on the ranch—I'm thinking the ranch would be where we put the families and they could still have access to the vineyard. We could have someone available to drive them over and give them a tour or let them help harvest or get the experience or have romantic candlelight dinners. It would be a pretty good undertaking but I just think—or we've been thinking— that it would be a good idea."

"I like it. I think you're right. I can run some numbers. I can get Amber to help me—we can probably have something worked up for you later this week. Maybe we could all meet then and discuss it further. I think we need to be clear on what exactly you would be giving up in doing this. Because you would be—you've got to have someone on hand all the time running the place. There could be headaches with it. But, yeah, I think it would be great. We've got the resources to hire plenty of people—someone to manage it, someone to run all of it. So, yeah, I'd be on board with it, I think. I'll run the numbers and get back to you on it."

Todd grinned. "Good. I don't know—I kind of think Granddaddy would be happy with that. He wanted great-grandkids. Do you get that, Morgan? I think he realized that all this needed to have someone to retain it, to enjoy it—not just work it but to live on it and love it. I think he missed when we were kids—the sound of us running up and down these vines…our laughter…our fun. I think he missed that."

Morgan wasn't sure how he felt about this conversation. He missed the way it had been when he had been growing up and he and his granddaddy seemed to get along better. "You might be right. But he still didn't have a right to try to force us to do this."

Todd shrugged. "Maybe not but what's done is done and we all know that we take what we've got and we work with it. And this is what we've got—this is what you've got. Now, let it go and let it ride. Figure it out—I'm eager to see what the numbers show."

As Morgan headed back to the house, he knew he would get home long before Amber. She was going to be shopping all evening—at least, he assumed. When he got home, he closed himself up in his office and started working on the numbers. He had never envisioned guests on the property. Not overnight guests. But he was in the resort and hotel industry business and he could see the possibilities.

What he couldn't see was letting go of the feelings inside him.

CHAPTER SEVENTEEN

Penny called the next day while Morgan and Amber were pulling numbers together on the vineyard project and both pretending everything was back to normal. Morgan took the call.

"Morgan, this is Penny. I've got the wedding reception all lined out. I've got invitations ordered and they're heading out to all the friends and family around. It's going to be a shindig like we did for your brothers, just a close-knit event to celebrate for you guys. We're going to do it week after next. How's that sound?"

Morgan understood Penny; she was a force to be

reckoned with and for the woman to pull together a reception within two weeks, with guests invited—he was not going to tell her no. Besides, he wanted to get it over with, have that behind them. Pulling the wool over everybody he had grown up around and knew around him didn't quite sit well with him. Both Todd and Wade had told him they hadn't enjoyed that part of it, either, but for them it worked out. And they hadn't been lying to their friends.

Morgan knew for him it wouldn't be that way. He just hoped they never found out the ridiculousness of the reason he and Amber had married.

He hung the phone up after they ended the call and he had agreed to everything that Penny said, making the old woman happy—not that him disagreeing would've made any difference. He laughed when he hung up. He did like Penny; she had been around for a very long time and that was just her way. He also knew that she had adored his granddaddy and his grandmother, and she felt the same way about Talbert. They had grown up together as kids and even though they weren't blood relatives, she felt like it.

Amber studied him as he hung up the phone. She

had a quirk to her lips and looking at her, he smiled. She wore a pretty, soft, sage-colored shirt that made her eyes dance and showed off her feminine curves. Though he tried not to notice all that, it was getting harder and harder every day not to. And she also smelled really good; he had noticed that when she leaned over to point out some numbers to him earlier. She was starting to distract him. And instead of sitting here in this office with her today, he was thinking that he wanted to take her somewhere, to show her around a little bit. *He was losing his mind.*

"Whoever that was sounded like they had plans."

"Oh, yeah, it was Penny. Whether we want one or not, we're having a wedding reception in two weeks. That okay with you? Because I have to warn you, whether it is or not, it's a done deal. Penny—she's like a tornado: she gets an idea in her head and she'll tear through everything until it gets done."

"Well, I have nowhere else to go, nowhere else to run. I'm here for the duration so that's fine with me. It will be actually kind of fun. Keep me from getting bored."

"So you're bored? Didn't you go shopping all day

yesterday or all afternoon at least?"

"Did I ever tell you that shopping was not my favorite thing to do in the world? I went shopping because I needed some clothes. But I also enjoyed seeing the country. Texas Hill Country's beautiful and Fredericksburg is interesting. We ate at some little German restaurant and I had some really good food. And I found some really cute clothes—many of them were unique. I don't know if you noticed the jeans I have on—they have handcrafted edging at the bottom. Hand sewn. And see the little flower on the edge down there? That's also hand sewn. Couldn't find that just anywhere, but in Fredericksburg you can find almost anything. I even got me a pair of bell-bottoms with tassels on the edge."

"No kidding? You don't really look like the tassel kind of gal."

She smiled and her eyes narrowed a bit. "Well, Morgan McCoy, you don't know everything there is to know about me. Just because you fished me out of the ocean doesn't mean you know everything."

He crossed his arms and studied her, smiling. "I believe you're probably right about that, Mrs. McCoy.

Maybe I need to change that. How about you put on those bell-bottoms, as you called them, with tassels on the edge on tonight and I'll take you out?" *He had most definitely lost his mind.*

"Seriously?" She seemed uncertain but excited.

"Yeah, I mean, you realize there's places all over this area that I can take you. But let's go to Gruene."

"Gruene? You mean like Gruene, the little town…"

"Yeah, Gruene, the little town with the oldest dance hall in Texas. We'll go to the Gristmill for dinner—it's a unique experience—and then we'll go to the dance hall and I'll twirl you around a little bit and maybe you can fill me in on some of the things I don't know about you. Like those bell-bottoms with the tassels that you are so crazy about, obviously."

Her eyes brightened and sparkled and made his heart lighter just looking at her.

"Well, I think that's an offer I just can't pass up. I've never been dancing at the oldest honky-tonk in Texas. Oh, wait—it's not a honky-tonk. It's a dance hall, right?"

"You got it right—dance hall. And it might surprise you that growing up, I danced there with my brothers a lot. Luckenbach is down in there, too—a little bit out of the way but it's just a little hole in the wall. I'm taking you to the dance hall."

"What are we waiting on? You and I both know that the numbers on that B&B are great. This place was made for visitors."

"You're right. We've got everything we need to give to my brothers. To make their day. Now let's make our day. You go get ready. I'll meet you back down here in an hour. Is that enough time or you need two or three more?"

She laughed. "An hour is fine, buddy."

"Then time starts now. Meet you in an hour."

She spun on her heel and almost raced toward the door. She looked over her shoulder and winked at him. "This is going to be fun. And just think—you won't have to rescue me out of the water. Now, you may have to rescue me on the dance floor. I never said I was a good dancer."

He winked at her. "You're safe because believe it or not, I am. Though it's been a loooong time since I two-stepped or waltzed, I believe I can remember how it's done."

"Then I'll see you in forty-five minutes." And with that, she was gone.

He stared after her, his pulse racing and his heart thumping a little faster. He realized that he couldn't wait for forty-five minutes to be up because he would see Amber again. Within a span of a couple of hours, he'd be holding her in his arms and whirling her around the dance floor. He realized, at that moment, that nothing had ever sounded so good.

* * *

The Gristmill was lovely. By the time they arrived, it was dark and the little town of Gruene—a German spelling, she believed—was busy. It was definitely a tourist attraction. There were shops all around and people everywhere. Music played in the wooden building that was pretty much the cornerstone of the small town. They had to walk past it, along a beautiful, wide brick path lit by soft light, to the Gristmill, which was ancient-looking and situated on the edge of the river. Someone greeted them as they arrived at the entrance of the building; they took their name, told them their seats would be ready in just a few moments, and asked them to wait in the courtyard, which was to the left.

People were milling around; someone sat on a small stage, playing the guitar and singing. People stood around or sat at picnic tables, enjoying a glass of wine or water or soda. People were just enjoying themselves, chatting, and didn't seem to be in a hurry. It was a very relaxed atmosphere and crowded. She looked at the building. It was tall, with exposed brick and old wooden doors leading inside; she could see a bar out one side on the exterior, with a dining area to the side with picnic tables on it.

"This is a very interesting place. I can't believe I've never been here although, like I said, I stayed pretty much in my own little world. I've always heard about it but just never driven down here."

"It's a great place. It's always busy like this. I mean, it slows in the winter some. Coming into October, it's cooler but actually a great time to come because you can imagine how hot it can be out here waiting in the summer. Now it's extremely pleasant. More locals will come as the tourists thin out. It can be a nightmare down here—it's such a small area, with so much shopping—but that doesn't deter people. I don't come here very often anymore but I'd thought you'd enjoy it. You can sit over there in that little dining area at the picnic tables, or inside the building there's a varying degree of seating situations—nice tables, some secluded areas—but it can be pretty crowded at times. I've requested a table at the far corner overlooking the river. I think you'll enjoy it."

"Oh, you called in a reservation?"

"Yes, I did. She's just making sure that everything's ready."

"You went all out, I see, Mr. McCoy."

"Well, I wasn't going to take you out for an evening and not go all out. I want you to enjoy yourself. Especially since you're going to let me in on all the secrets of your past and let me get to know you better."

She laughed. "I see you have an ulterior motive."

"Maybe. You intrigue me. You're a woman who decided to marry me on a whim. That in itself is shocking to me. And you're not a greedy person—I can tell that—so, yeah, I'm curious."

This pleased her. She could hardly believe that he

was actually curious about her. Her heart had ramped up at the idea that he truly wanted to know about her. She tried not to get ahead of herself and just to enjoy the evening. And that was exactly what she planned to do; it was just too lovely not to.

The young lady came back and took them to their seat. They weaved their way through the maze of tables and varying dining rooms. They were seated on a candlelit deck, with overhanging plants and shrubs giving them a bit of a secluded spot. The sound of the flowing river below them helped ease the sound of the conversations all around.

"This is lovely. You may have to bring me back here. I may fall in love with this place."

"I can do that."

They ordered and enjoyed a great evening.

"You never talk about yourself. Tell me about your parents. Where do they live? Do they know you married me?"

She hesitated, gathering her thoughts. She'd shared with others about her past but not many people knew. Still, sharing with him seemed so personal. "My parents died in a car crash when I was in the seventh grade."

He covered her hand with his. "I'm so sorry. All this time, and you didn't say anything and yet, you know how it felt to lose your parents. Are you okay? Who took care of you?"

She tried to smile, while holding back the sudden burn of tears. She would not get emotional. "My great aunt," she said, huskily. She collected herself. "Unfortunately, I wasn't blessed with a granddaddy who wanted to care for me like your granddaddy did for you and your brothers. My great aunt was the CEO of a major company in Dallas and never married because she chose her career instead. She sent me off to boarding school almost immediately and that is where I lived for the next five years. And then college."

"I am so sorry. Did you not go home any, like for holidays?"

"Not much. I did a couple of times, but she was always traveling and it never worked. It made me miss Mom and Dad all the more and the way life used to be. So, I stayed at school and sometimes went home with a friend. But I learned to be grateful for the short time

I'd had them and the time when life was perfect and I've moved forward."

He stared at her, the warmth of his hand so very comforting to her. For the first time in so very long her heart ached for her parents. But looking at him, she felt a small hope for what could be her future.

It was foolish, so foolish.

By the time they finished their meal and had walked out of the building, she was touched when Morgan took her hand in his again.

He smiled. "Hope you don't mind."

Her heart pounded. "No, not at all. After all, you know all my secrets now." She couldn't help but tease and it helped hide the feeling of the out-of-body experience she was having at the moment.

They strolled down the brick path toward the dance hall. She could hear the old Texas country music coming from the dance hall. Someone was playing a harmonica; there were guitars and someone playing piano. People stood around on the grass and under the humongous trees that filled the yard; they were lit by spotlights that shone up into the massive tree branches. All in all, it was a hugely romantic feeling and despite all the people milling around, there was a coziness to it. They paused along with others along the edge of the dance hall and watched everyone inside through the screen that acted as windows.

She could see that on one end was a larger stage and on the other end was a smaller stage and that's where the band was playing tonight. Across the dance hall was a pool table; people were enjoying themselves, playing pool, while others sat around the edges of the dance hall, at the tables, and enjoyed the music.

"This band—they're not as big as some of the others. Garth Brooks has played on that bigger stage at the other end down there. He was here just recently and this whole yard was full—it was standing room only as far as you could see. Stoney LaRue, George Straight—George Straight has been here many times—and, of course, Willie Nelson—just everybody tries to come here. It's really kind of different because some of those guys can fill up huge stadiums and they come here to this little tiny place and like to play because Gruene Hall is just Gruene Hall."

"I love it. And I'm not even a great dancer. I haven't really danced a lot but I can't wait to go in there and dance. You sure you're good?"

To her surprise, he laid his arm across her shoulders and drew her in to his side. "I hope I can remember what I'm doing because I sure do want to dance well with you. I need to impress you."

Morgan McCoy didn't need to impress anyone. And yet as she looked up at him, she almost felt as though he meant what he was saying.

CHAPTER EIGHTEEN

Morgan wanted to kiss Amber. He had wanted to kiss Amber all night. She had been on his mind all day. That was why he hadn't been able to resist asking her to come here tonight. And as he looked at her in the soft light of the mini lights from up above the tree lines and the light filtering from inside the dance hall, he bent his head and almost kissed her before he pulled back.

"Maybe we better go inside or I'll be kissing you here on the sidewalk." He had never been one to not speak his mind. "And we both know that's not a good thing."

"Or maybe you could kiss me right here."

Her bold words startled him and caused his heart to hammer faster in his chest. It wasn't something he was accustomed to. She had caused him to be off-balance ever since they first met. And it hadn't changed since. "I could but I'm afraid if I start kissing you, I might not stop and this isn't exactly the kind of place I want to do that. Even though it is romantically lit, it is very public."

"Then lead the way and let's go in there and dance."

He took her hand again and led her down the brick pathway and around the corner to the far side of the building where the entrance was. When he got there, he gave them his name; he had already called ahead and made arrangements. They smiled and took him to a table, over to the left of the musicians. It was a good table—easy access to the dancefloor and close enough up front where they had great access to the musicians. The truth, though, was Gruene Hall wasn't very big and no matter where you sat you had great access to both the dancefloor and the musicians. He just liked this table; he remembered this table from the days of his youth when he and his brothers would gather around this table and use it as their command center as they pretty much took over this dance hall and danced with every pretty girl they could convince to dance with them. He hadn't thought about that in years. They had been young and rambunctious and young bucks. And they had loved to dance. They had all worn boots out on this dancefloor and many dancefloors across the Hill Country area. He hadn't done that in years.

Oh, he had been dancing but he had been dancing at country clubs and ballrooms at resorts and black-tie events. But to actually wear jeans and boots and a shirt and relax completely—no, he hadn't done that in a very long time.

They ordered glasses of wine and sipped on them as they listened to the singer belt out a love song. People were on the floor, dancing, doing a slow two-step.

"Would you like to dance?"

She smiled at him and stood. "I thought you would never ask."

He laughed again as he took her hand and led her out onto the floor. To her surprise, he spun her and then pulled her into his arms.

She gasped, "I wasn't expecting that."

He grinned, breathing in the scent of her, burying his nose in her soft hair just enough to enjoy feeling her against him and letting the scent engulf him. "I hope to surprise you all evening."

Her arm went around him. He liked the way it felt around his waist; he liked the way she looked up at him, bringing his mouth closer to her temple. Unable to stop himself, he lightly brushed his lips across her temple. Her eyes widened. "Hope you don't mind. Couldn't help myself."

"I think I'm going to enjoy this evening very much."

"I already am. And you know what? Don't know if you noticed it, but you're dancing." He had been leading them in the two-step—shuffle two steps side, back two steps, side, back—and she had been going with him, the rhythm to the music easy.

"I see I am. You're a very good dancer—you're leading me and I didn't even know I was doing it."

"You're a natural. It's not me—you just took with the beat and that's what it does: a slow two-step."

"I think," she looked up at him, "that we just kind of work well together."

He stared at her. They did work well together. "You're right. But don't forget we're not working right now—we're dancing."

She smiled and a soft laugh escaped her. "So we are. So we are."

* * *

They had a wonderful time dancing. Several times she thought he wanted to kiss her but he didn't. Though her heart hammered and her pulse raced and the desire to stay in his arms forever had taken over and made her into a dreamy mess, Amber held onto her composure and just tried to enjoy the evening without putting too many unrealistic hopes on what it might lead to. In her dreams, she wanted it to lead to a life with Morgan McCoy, forever and ever. But even in the short time they'd been together, she was beginning to worry that could never happen.

But tonight was her night and she held on to him and laughed and flirted and teased and just let it be what it was: a wonderful night between a couple who obviously had an attraction to each other. And that was it. No other expectations. It was a lie and she knew it, but it was her way of getting through the night without allowing herself to get too serious or to deceive herself—at least not too much, anyway.

After about the tenth dance, they were both hot and she was even a little bit sweaty. They had danced so much—even a couple of line dances that she hadn't known and he had surprised her with the fact that they were oldies and he did know them. Then they sat down and watched the younger crowd, the twenty-somethings, do a couple of line dances.

He looked at her, grinning. "Those I don't know, as you can tell. I know the Cotton-Eyed Joe and a couple others from back in the day. Even my granddaddy knew the Cotton-Eyed Joe. Matter of fact, my granddaddy taught me the Cotton-Eyed Joe. So I'm just passing it on to you tonight."

She was holding his arm and they were sitting close on the stools. She leaned forward and laid her head on his shoulder briefly and then looked up at him. "I think you're amazing and even though you had an ill-spent youth, I'm really glad you did because this is so much fun."

"I have to admit, it felt good to let myself relax like this tonight. It's been a long time. Want anything else to drink?"

"Could they give me some water maybe?"

"Yes, they can." He smiled and waved the waitress over and ordered two glasses of water with lemon.

It was just a small thing but the fact that he remembered that she liked lemon in her water gave her a boost.

"I think you should do this more often."

His jaw tightened and his eyes got a faraway look in them for a moment. Then he lifted his shoulders slightly. "Maybe. But I have a lot of business. Have a lot of responsibilities."

She toyed with the napkin and smiled at the waitress as waters appeared before them. She was thoughtful as she decided to just go ahead and speak her mind again. Though she didn't want to mess up the evening at all. "But you have people. You're very good at hiring excellent people."

"We've talked about that and yes, we do. But like my granddaddy, I have a control issue. I like to be in control. I like the feeling of accomplishment that I get when I know that what happened was…"

"Your doing?"

He stared at her. "That does sound arrogant, doesn't it?"

It was her turn to lift her shoulders in a shrug and she gave a small smile. "A little. Yes, you make the major decisions and you are the one it all revolves around, but you do have a great team. Who bring you great opportunities, call your attention to them, help you develop them, help you run the resorts. I get why you say it's you and I understand that because it really is. But is what you sacrifice worth it?"

He took a drink of his water then set it down on the table and placed both hands around it. He stared at the people on the dancefloor.

She could see his mind whirling in thought as he had that contemplative expression on his face. She loved that look. She was crazy.

He looked back at her. "I don't know. Maybe I lost sight of some very important things and maybe I need to take a closer look at that."

It wasn't the answer she had hoped for and she understood it probably wasn't the answer his grandfather was hoping for when he had done this, but it was a start. She smiled. "I think that's a great idea. Then again, you're full of them."

She laughed and he shook his head. "You want to dance? One thing I know for certain—I'm not ready for this night to end and you still have lessons coming, young lady, because before the night's over, we're going to learn that line dance right there."

She watched the fairly aggressive line dance going on. "I'm game. And what do you mean, we're going to be sore? We're barely in our thirties. We're not ancient. Besides, I know some dancing grannies who can do that right there and then some, so don't be getting all uppity there and assume anything."

He laughed as he took her hand and led her onto the dancefloor. Personally, she preferred the ones where he held her in her arms and snuggled close. But this was fun too.

CHAPTER NINETEEN

The next several days passed pretty uneventfully. They seemed closer, even though he had pulled away a little in the couple of days after their dance. But she had half expected that because Morgan was extremely conflicted and she understood that he was a very thoughtful person and that he never left any rocks unturned and their relationship would be one of great contemplation and thought. He spent several hours with his brothers, locked in the study, as they discussed the preliminary plans for whether they would go through with doing a small inn or bed-and-breakfast on the properties.

She spent time with the puppies. They were fat as butterballs; it was amazing how a week and a half could grow a puppy. The mother was darling and she was now getting around almost without a limp, which was a good thing. Thankfully, Allie had agreed to come over and see Goldie and decide whether they were going to take the dog. Allie and Wade were pretty certain that a beautiful sweet Golden Retriever mix would be the perfect addition to the property. And the puppies…they figured they could either keep them considering there were only four or probably find good homes for them because they came from a good mixture of dog.

Today, one of the puppies was a little bit listless and had a warm nose. Amber decided to run him into town to see Ash. The clinic was open and when she called, his receptionist told her to bring him in any time. She was very grateful to have a vet in the family. She left Morgan a note, not wanting to interrupt the meeting, and took the puppy, reassuring the worried-looking mother that she would bring her puppy back to her. She went out and loaded up in the truck. As she drove into town, she realized that in such a very short time, she had really grown to love the area. She loved the sagebrush and the mesquite and the occasional oak tree. She loved the rocks and the cactus and the occasional burst of lingering wildflowers that, as the weather cooled, would quickly disappear. They were hanging on by the strongest roots and she expected that she could even drive this way in the next hour and they would be gone, but most likely they would last another couple of weeks. And then it would be only the tanned-toned dried grass and the bare trees. But even in that, there was beauty that the Texas Hill Country had that no other places in Texas really had.

Oh, she loved central Texas. Near Houston, when you drove down I-45, especially toward Dallas, when you got into the more rural areas and the cities and the constant concrete and outdoor malls gave way to rolling pastures and beautiful oak trees and cows dotting the pasture, there was an amazing beauty there, too. Both places were gorgeous in their own way. Texas itself was just an amazing state; the wide expanse made a person think long and hard about how big life was. And how different. There was a little bit of everything for everyone and she just liked that. But

Hill Country—she wondered whether the appeal of it to her was that Morgan was here.

She knew that if and when she went back to Houston, that when she left McCoy Stonewall Enterprises to go out on her own and use the money that she was getting from this agreement between her and him, that she would miss him. Even knowing that he was in the same city, if she chose to open her business, whatever it was she decided to do, she knew that probably knowing he was near and not being able to see him even from afar was not going to sit well. She was going to have to seriously come up with a plan on what she was going to do after she wasn't married to Morgan any longer. It was not something she wanted to think about.

And so she didn't; she drove into town. Stonewall was a tiny place but it was cute. When she passed through and then drove on into the country where Ash had his clinic, she thought about the puppy and decided she might take a puppy with her. She would take a part of this brief moment of time, these three months, and she would keep it with her.

She glanced down at the puppy beside her, laid her

hand on it, and gently rubbed its tiny head. "You need to get well, little fella, because I'm going to keep you. I'm going to keep you with me forever."

Lynette greeted her at the door. There were people waiting and she felt a little bit odd when she was led past them and into a waiting room. "I don't need to go in front of those people. I can wait."

"Oh, you're not. They're waiting on their dogs. They have someone else with them and the puppies, well, I mean the cows are out back, so there's nobody else inside the waiting room. It's a large animal day, so you just come in here and be comfortable. Ash normally has small animal day on a different day than when he's out back, but in emergencies or when family or friends need him or when there's a need, he takes whoever it is. He's good that way. He's very accommodating. He's a great guy. How are you and Morgan doing?"

"Oh, good." There was a little bit of an uncomfortable silence because she really didn't know what else to say. People who didn't know why they were married and thought that they were truly over the hill in love with each other—it was a little bit of an ordeal still and did make her nerves rattle a bit.

Lynette cuddled the puppy she was holding, touched its warm nose and cooed. "Poor baby. He does have a fever, I think, but it's probably nothing. You know, everybody's hoping Morgan decides to stay here a little bit more than he used to. And we're glad to have you. We've all been curious about who Morgan would decide to marry one day. He's a little bit different from the other boys and, well, we just thought that he would show up with some model on his arm or a very glossy type woman with extravagant tastes and probably someone who didn't have an appreciation for the land and the life we all live."

Amber, again, wasn't sure what to say. She cleaned up pretty good when she put heels on and her business attire or the few times she dressed up; she recalled the night in Kauai when she wore the dress that Mrs. Beasley had arranged for her. She had, in her own mind, looked nice. But she was a long way from being a glossy type model; that was laughable. "Well, I hope I didn't disappoint everybody too bad."

Lynette laughed heartily. "Oh, honey, no. You are refreshing. You're the buzz about town. Everybody's talking about you and how wonderful you are for him and how unexpected. Seeing you with him gave everybody a hope that maybe he was coming back to his roots. That maybe he hadn't forgotten us all. You know, his granddaddy, I think, was really worried about that. He, like Morgan, loved the resort and hotel business when he went into it. I don't know—the excitement of it or the adrenaline probably got pumping, and when J.D. would talk about buying a new resort and remodeling it and getting it up to the standards of the McCoy Stonewall Enterprises Resort and Hotel Division, you could see the pride in his eyes. He had pride in his ranch and he had pride in the vineyard, but the resort and hotel business was different.

"I guess because it was more of a worldwide endeavor, maybe. I don't know. But we lost him for a little while, too. He got him an apartment in Houston and spent a lot of time there. Then he handed it over to Morgan and he came home. He seemed to be, in those years, settled and happy, and he and Wade worked with the ranch mostly. He completely went back to his roots there on that land. And I don't expect Morgan to do that, but just seeing you and that he fell in love with a woman his granddaddy would approve of wholeheartedly just makes my heart swell. And makes me happy. I just wanted to tell you that.

"And I'm coming to Penny's wedding reception that she's throwing for you. I was excited to get the invitation. I think there will be a huge crowd there of well-wishers. Everybody was at the one Penny threw for Wade and Todd, and I know they'll all be there for Morgan. Partly out of curiosity about you because, unlike me, most people haven't gotten to see you, so they're going to come and welcome you with open arms. I just want to assure you that, so no more worrying. I didn't mean to worry you. I can see it in your eyes."

"Thank you. I'm not worried." What a lie she was telling, because now she was more worried than ever. These people were going to welcome her with open arms—what a relief—but then she was going to be gone and he was going to be divorced, and what were they going to think of her then? How disappointed were they going to be then?

She was holding the puppy snuggled up against her

jaw when Ash came through the door. He was smiling and looked about as friendly as a guy could be. She had a feeling he did a booming business here in this area. He was perfect for what he did: personable, energetic. And he was single. The man probably had women falling all over him. He had boyish good looks; his deep-brown eyes sparkled, and his smile and his curly hair just were a pleasant experience to look at.

She couldn't help smiling back at him. "Hi. We're back."

"I see that. I hear you brought my patient back to me. Little fella is probably just going through a little stomach problem or something. Here, let me take him." He reached for the puppy and she handed him over. Their hands touched but there were no sparks like she felt when Morgan's hands touched her. But she already knew that there were no sparks when this good-looking, gorgeous guy smiled at her at all. She was a goner when it came to falling for Morgan and she knew that.

"I hope it's just a stomach problem and nothing else. I know I should've just called but I needed to get out of the house and I thought that if you could look at him, it would be just a relief to me."

He set the puppy on the table and felt around on it and gently touched its belly and then looked at its face and opened its mouth and looked inside. He shot her a sideways glance. "So you're doing okay? I see Morgan didn't come with you. I guess he's busy?" He went back to looking over the puppy.

"I'm doing good. Yeah, Morgan's busy this morning. He and Wade and Todd are going over some stuff, so I brought the puppy myself. And it's not like it's hard to travel around here. I'm used to Houston traffic—this is wide-open spaces."

He straightened up, picked the puppy up, petted it a few times, and then handed it back to her. "You're right about that—we're definitely not Houston and I'm very glad about that. Puppy's fine—I think he's just having a little bit of a stomach issue. I'll give him a little prescription to help with that and you can take him home to watch him. But I'm glad you brought him in. It's good to see you. Penny tells me we're going to be having a wedding reception pretty soon like we did for Wade and Todd. My grandad Talbert—have you met my granddad?"

"No, I haven't had the privilege."

"Well, my granddaddy, like we say, he's been watching and he is really getting antsy. He is really happy about J.D.'s grandsons getting married. And I have to say, they all seem to be happy." He studied her closely. "But am I crazy or does there seem to be something not quite right about you and Morgan?"

She was startled by his question. "What do you mean? We're fine."

"I hope so. I just—well, to be honest, I kind of have a sense about people and animals. I don't know, maybe it's because I'm a vet and I can sense whether animals are feeling good and happy or feeling bad and upset, and sometimes I can feel that about people, too. The other day when you and Morgan came in, I didn't quite feel as much newlywed exuberance as much as I felt like I should be feeling. Is everything okay?"

He was really stepping across a barrier or maybe he was just intuitive like he said, but she wasn't really sure this was an area that he should be stepping into. Bothered, she cuddled the puppy and met his concerned gaze head on. "Do you normally question your married clients about their marital status?"

His eyes widened and his expression took on the appearance of dismay. "No, I didn't mean it like—I mean, I didn't mean to step into your business. It's just Morgan—we all go way back and I just…I don't know why I asked that question. I'm just concerned. I'm sorry. I apologize. You can tell Morgan he can come up here and slug me if he wants to. I don't know why I was asking."

She didn't either. Of course, they had just been getting along then and everything was new and they hadn't gone dancing and hadn't shared any actual time getting used to the fact that they were married at that point. Even though that wasn't even barely a week ago…a little over a week—time was muddling up on her. In some respects, it seemed as though it were flying; in others, it seemed as if it were creeping along. She didn't know what to say to this concerned cousin.

"I'm not going to mention it to Morgan, as far as a matter of being angry. But I'll tell him you were concerned. We're fine. When we came in here, we were worried about the puppies and the dog. We had been out riding." *Why was she explaining this to Ash? Was he like a dog whisperer—was she wishing she could tell him her problems and he could figure everything out for her?* She needed to just keep her mouth shut and go on. It wasn't as if he found him a wife that she was going to be prying into his business. No, she had come in here with the thought that he was someone she could trust with her dog—not with her secrets of her marital complications. "Thank you for your concern, really, and we hope we see you at the wedding reception. Are you bringing a date?"

There, payback.

"No, I'm not bringing a date. I'm not going to give my granddaddy any more reason to think that he can start pressing me for marriage. He's already hinting."

"Have you ever thought that maybe he raised you and he's looking forward to having some little children of yours running around?"

"Maybe." He laughed. "Just like J.D. was looking forward to having great-grandkids by his bunch and it didn't happen. I'm sad to say, but with all of y'all married now, it's going to happen—probably pretty soon. I'm stepping on a line again—didn't mean to step out of line again."

Maybe she was taking his question a little too

personal. "Well, just remember that your granddaddy loves you and he probably can't help but want great-grandchildren. He's probably old enough where that's a great expectation of his. You're about Morgan's age, so it's not too much to ask. Do you not date?"

"So I guess now that I opened this can of worms, you have the right to ask me questions about my personal life." His eyes twinkled.

"I believe you're right—you did open the can of worms. Are you just too busy around here to not go find a significant other or do you have an aversion to commitment or what's the deal?"

He put his hands on his hips and studied her. "I did not realize that Morgan had married a fireball. I guess maybe I'm a little bit commitment phobic. You know, it takes a long time to get through vet school and I made it through vet school without getting tied down...but I didn't do it intentionally. I was just determined to get my degree and that's what I did. And now I've got my clinic open—been open for a few years now and I'm settling in. So maybe I'll be ready pretty soon."

She gave him a skeptical look. "Or maybe you're

going to get settled in your ways and then you're never going to give your granddaddy what he wants. You, Ash McCoy, probably need to be open-minded about this. I'm on your granddaddy Talbert's side. Maybe you need to rethink that and bring a date to the wedding reception."

"Maybe we will agree not to step on each other's toes when it comes to our personal lives. I wholeheartedly apologize for my misstep a while ago." He grinned and she laughed; she couldn't help it.

"I like you, Ash, and I'm not going to agree to anything. You made that bed—now I may have to get with your sister, Caroline, and we may need to hatch a plan on how to get you married."

He looked completely shocked. "Do not tell me you're a matchmaker. You are not going to join up with my sister. If she gets into my personal life, you do not even understand what kind of havoc she can cause."

She grinned. "Oh, I've spent time with Caroline. I understand completely what kind of havoc your sister could bestow if she wanted to. She is a force to be reckoned with."

He cocked his head to one side and then shook his head. "Amber, I believe you are too. And, you know what? I take back everything I said because I do believe my cousin has met his match."

His words settled on her heart and made her feel good. She sure wished she was his match—she wanted to be Morgan's match. Wanted it more than anything in the world. But she sure didn't tell Ash that. Nope, no one would know her secret. And the day she left, she wondered what people like Ash would think. He would know that he was correct in wondering about her and Morgan. The man was good but she wasn't going to tell him that. "Thanks for looking at my puppy. I guess I better go home now."

"I guess you better. I'll follow you out there and I'll write you a prescription for the puppy. Actually, we have it on the shelf, so it won't be a big deal. Give it to the puppy before he eats and he will be fine."

"Thank you very much. And like I said, I'll be watching for you and a date coming to the reception."

He laughed and opened the door for her. "I'm afraid you'll be waiting for a long time. I'm coming alone."

She headed through the door and into the front and

wondered what it was about these McCoy men—and Caroline, too—that made them so commitment phobic when it came to finding the person to spend the rest of their lives with. *Why did it have to come down to the fact that their grandparents had to try to force them into doing something?* Far as she could figure, it must be a McCoy trait that they'd all gotten. *Or...* She wondered whether it could be something from the fact that Ash's parents and Morgan's parents had been killed in the same plane crash. Both sets of kids had lost their parents and their granddaddies had raised them. *Could that have a lingering effect on them?*

It was something she hadn't really thought about and it was probably something that she was wrong about. But, still, she wondered and as she drove toward home, her curiosity grew.

CHAPTER TWENTY

Morgan had gone over the numbers with his brothers and they had started the plans for a preliminary search of what type of building and small resort they were going to open. He kept calling it a resort when he meant bed-and-breakfast. He wasn't used to the idea of a bed-and-breakfast. No, he was used to doing things big, so going small was alien to him. Still, he liked the idea of something small here. So he had contacted Mrs. B and had his team researching dude ranches across Texas and what kind of businesses they were running.

They should have that in the next week or so, and

then they would talk about it some more. They were going to bring Ginny and Allie in on that now that they had settled in on financially that it was doable and would be more than likely profitable; they had the numbers to back it up. He had just wanted to make sure it wasn't just some sentimental thing. He liked sentimental but he liked profitable better.

Mrs. B had been glad to hear from him, not that they didn't talk once or twice a week, but she was always asking about Amber and how things were. He had a feeling that deep down Mrs. B was hoping that he and Amber would stay together. He didn't want to think about all that—didn't want to think about the fact that they wouldn't stay together. He was stubborn.

* * *

All the girls went shopping again a few days before the wedding reception using it as an excuse to go look for gorgeous dresses and hang out together. It was something that Amber thoroughly enjoyed and the fact that the four of them got along so well really was a miracle and caused her heart to ache really hard. So much of this journey had been a surprise. She was such a loner—had kept to herself for so long—and suddenly she belonged to a group of people. She had girlfriends. She didn't have to go to coffee by herself; she didn't just go to work and leave and then go home and hole up most of the time. She was enjoying herself. They kidded and did things from *Pretty Woman* as they all came out of the dressing room wearing different dresses; everyone would give it a nod or a thumbs-up or give it a thumbs-down, and then they laughed. Afterward, when they all had gorgeous dresses, they went for a late lunch. Well, it was more like an afternoon meal because it had taken them awhile at the fancy, awesome boutique that they had gone to. Their hubbies had all insisted and Caroline had jumped at the chance to shop. The woman was a mixture of downhome Texas gal and pure wealthy high society Texan. It was a very odd combination and one that Amber enjoyed immensely. Especially when she would tell them about the escapades of her teasing the county sheriff, Jesse James.

She and the sheriff obviously had a weird relationship. Amber would never speed when a cop was around but Caroline acted as if it were a fun pastime. It was funny; the cop would stop her and from what it sounded like, it was almost as if they teased each other. Of course, Caroline thoroughly explained that she didn't get out of hand and that she was always in control. And that it had only happened a few times. But there was definitely something there between the two, and from the looks that Amber shared with Allie and Ginny, they all wondered whether there was more to it than even Caroline realized. Sounded a lot like Jesse James might have a crush on Caroline. Or vice versa. But to hear Caroline get all high and mighty talking about it, it was hard to tell whether she actually did.

The day after they got the dresses, Wade called and invited everybody over to the ranch. He had an announcement he wanted all the brothers there for.

She and Morgan loaded up and rode over. They had been slightly avoiding each other but when they were summoned like this, there wasn't that much avoidance that could be had inside a pickup truck. He was gorgeous today as usual, still wearing those jeans that hugged his hips and the shirts that fit him to a T and showed off his muscular physique. And that clean-shaven jaw of his and that luscious dark hair... With sunshades on, the man looked a little bit dangerous. She knew what those eyes looked like behind those shades. She told herself to stop and she stared straight ahead. All she could think about was at the engagement party they would get to dance again. Things had been really off since their last dance at the Gruene Hall. And the kiss. The kiss that still caused her blood pressure to skyrocket.

"Not sure what my brother's calling us over here for but he had a really odd sound in his voice when he called. I think it's something real important."

"I wonder what it is, too. Allie didn't say anything yesterday when we were shopping. Although, right before we ate, she said she didn't feel great. It's one reason we came on home. We were all glad we found our dresses but we didn't want to linger, even though we had talked about maybe going to a movie or something."

"Well, I guess we'll find out pretty soon." He turned the engine off on the truck and hopped out the door and she met him at the front of the truck. He had been on his way to her side but she hadn't waited for him to come open the door. They walked inside the big ranch just as Todd and Ginny drove up, and they had barely gotten inside when the other couple joined them.

"Where are you, Wade?" Todd called as soon as they were in the kitchen.

"In the living room," Wade called.

They all followed Morgan down the hall and into the great room that they called the living room. Wade and Allie stood by the fireplace. Wade had his arm around Allie and they were smiling.

So much for it being something bad.

"Y'all come in." Wade motioned toward the chairs. "Allie and I have a pretty big announcement to make."

Anticipation rocked through the room and Amber, though new to the group, suddenly had a feeling she knew what was coming.

Everyone sat down. Morgan sat beside her on the couch; their knees brushed and their elbows touched as they sat there. She tried not to think how much she wished he would put his arm around her like Wade had his arm around Allie, and Todd had taken Ginny's hand. Ginny was grinning. It made Amber wonder whether maybe Ginny knew what was coming.

"So we called y'all as soon as we had confirmation but, Granddaddy would be very proud because, well, his wish is about to come true. We're expecting."

The room broke out in claps and Morgan grinned at her. He looked at Wade. "Well, there you go. Congratulations, you two. Granddaddy, the old coot, he got what he wanted."

"Man, that's awesome." Todd went over and gave his brother a big hug and then gave Allie a hug. Ginny followed, and Amber and Morgan got up too.

"I'm so excited for y'all." Amber hugged Allie. "I had this odd feeling yesterday that it could be a possibility but I just didn't believe or trust it, but I had hoped for you."

"I just didn't want to say anything until we knew for sure, but I'm so happy," Allie said. "I've already gone and told Mom, and she's ecstatic. I can see in her eyes how happy J.D. would be. These grandmothers, they do get excited about the thought of a grandchild. My mother is the grandmother and J.D. is the great-grandfather, but they just seem like they're both grandparents because J.D. pretty much raised the boys."

"It really does feel that way. But I know Mom and Dad would be so happy, too, so I know they're probably all celebrating right now." Wade kissed Allie's forehead. "I love you, girl. I'm so glad you're in my life."

Allie smiled into his eyes. "I'm so happy. And you're going to be the most wonderful daddy. I just can't wait."

"You're going to put me to shame, being an amazing mom. But I know one thing—I'm going to give you everything I've got to be the best daddy to our baby as I can be."

They all celebrated and chattered excitedly. As they were leaving, she glanced at Morgan and he seemed tense. She tried to ignore it; probably he was thinking about his granddaddy and the whole issue of being forced to marry but she was reluctant to bring it up. He hadn't taken to her pushing very well. And she understood his aggravation at his granddaddy; they had built McCoy Stonewall Enterprises together and being forced to save it by marriage was just really odd.

They got in the truck and he backed out and headed back toward his house. She saw his jaw tick and the frown line crease in his forehead. He was in deep thought.

She wanted to reach out and touch his hand but she didn't feel like she had a right to. But finally she couldn't help it; she reached out and touched his arm. "Are you okay?"

He glanced over at her, his eyes troubled. "I don't know what I am. I'm so mixed up these days. I feel like I fell in a rabbit hole and everything in my world is suddenly upside down." He stared straight ahead again.

"I can understand that. But you'll figure it out and we're halfway—over halfway there now. So just think about that. In about forty-five days, you'll be rid of me and everything will go back to normal."

She glanced at him when he didn't say anything. His jaw was even more tense than it had been. She didn't try to talk again until they reached the house. When they reached the deck he stopped her with a hand on her arm, sending tingling sensations rushing through her. She was hopeless.

"Wade was really happy."

"He was. And he's right—he and Allie are going to make amazing parents. And this place is going to be an amazing place to raise their family. But you already know that—you benefited from it growing up. I know your parents would be glad to know that at least one of their sons was carrying on the torch. And your granddaddy."

He let his thumb trace smoothly back and forth on her skin. His expression grew distant as he looked out over the land. She wondered what he was thinking about. When he looked back at her, there was a vulnerability in his eyes that twisted her heart.

Unable to stop herself, she lifted her arms and draped them over his shoulders and hugged him. "You're a good man, too, Morgan McCoy. And one day, when you're ready, you're going to make an amazing dad."

His hands had gone to her waist but his body was tense against hers as she had laid her head on his shoulder, just wanting to give him some comfort despite the fact that he didn't actually look like he welcomed it. And then, to her surprise, his hands went around her waist, slipped around her back, and then he stepped close so that he held her tightly.

"I would like to think so. But I don't know if it's going to be for me. Like I said before, I leave it to Wade and Todd. But I—I didn't tell you that I went to the ridge a week or so ago and I had a little talk with my granddaddy. About all this. I tried to understand. I tried to let go of it all and yet I still feel resentment at being forced into this. And, right now, holding you, I feel terrible because I feel resentment that you're in my life because my granddaddy took control and is trying to rule me."

What did she say to that? It was ridiculous the emotions that his words could fuel inside her. "I keep having to remind myself that the only reason I'm in your life is because your granddaddy forced you to do it. I don't know why I keep getting mixed up about that." She pushed away from him. Her heart ached and tears streamed out of her eyes. She brushed them away.

He was staring at her, confused. At this point, she didn't care that he had never seen her cry. She had tried not to, but something about the way he said that just got to her. Who was she kidding; they were halfway through this ordeal—and that's what it was: an ordeal. Because when it was all said and done, she was going to have a broken heart. It was already breaking right now. He resented that she was in his life, even though she was helping him. There was never going to be anything for them.

"I'm almost sorry that I agreed to help you out. Because I'm going to pay."

"Amber, come on. I didn't mean to hurt you like that."

Was he kidding? "Well, you did. I mean, yes, I'm getting money for being here. And you know what? The more I think about it, the more I hate that. This whole thing is about money. I'm an idiot, because I have told myself to keep that straight in my brain but, no, of course not—I haven't done that. I haven't kept that straight. And like a person who just can't learn a lesson, I have fallen in love with you. Yeah, stupid isn't it? No, don't say anything. Don't bother. I sold my soul to the devil when I signed onto this and I'm not one to give up.

"So, you know, I think I'll go to my room and kind of hole up there for a little while. You know what?

Better yet—yeah, I have, what, a week that I can take some time off and escape? I think I'll take that." She wrapped her arms around her waist. "Matter of fact, I'm going to go pack a bag. No, I'm not going to pack a bag. I have a McCoy credit card in my purse here. I'm going to go and get in the truck, and I'm going to go find me some place to hole up for a little while. Get my head on straight—let you get your head back on straight—and then maybe when I get back, I can have some distance. I'll have talked to myself very strongly and with any luck by tomorrow night when we have to put on a show for everybody and be a happily married couple, I'll be okay with it. How's that sound? That sound good to you? Because if I showed up there now, I'm sure we wouldn't look like a happily married couple. I'd look like a very angry disillusioned assistant who was a fool. And that wouldn't play well for all your friends and family who we're deceiving with a capital D."

She started walking toward the truck. He had left the keys in it. She'd had her purse; she had money and right now she planned to spend it. She was so hot that she figured if she didn't get control of herself, it might be dangerous for her to be behind the wheel. But she'd be okay; even if she had to drive five miles per hour, she was leaving this place right now.

"Amber, wait. Come on. This is not right. You're not a fool and you didn't sell your soul to the devil. We made a pact. It was a business agreement. That's all. You're not a fool. You're a very smart person. You're going to be glad to have it—"

She swung back toward him. "Always the businessman. No, this isn't an acquisition for a resort. Well, for you, it's the acquisition for hanging on to a bunch of resorts, but for me—well, surprise—I got into this because I had this crazy idea that I was already half in love with you. I agreed to this because I thought foolishly—yes, very foolishly—that I might have a shot with you if I could spend time alone with you. And I let my heart go crazy. And now I'm going to pay. You said it was a win-win situation when we got into it and it's very much a win-win situation for you. But for me, it's not. It was a losing situation from the very beginning. I was just too foolish to see it." She opened the door and climbed in.

He reached for the door but she yanked it closed

and slapped the lock. He stared at her through the window and she was glad the glass was up.

"Open the door, Amber. You're wrong. And you're too upset to drive."

"I'm not opening up and I'm completely in control. I'll drive slow but I'm leaving. I'm probably going to go to a spa or something. After all, I have all your money in my pocket and your credit card, and this is what this is all about. I'll have a ball. Be my last fling as Mrs. McCoy."

He raked a hand through his hair. His jaw was very tight. He was furious. But she could also see that he felt terrible. She might be making too much of this. But she didn't think so. "I'll text you when I get where I'm going and let you know I'm safe. Just so you don't worry. But I'm not going to tell you where I'm at. Of course, I'm sure that you can get your guys who do all your research for you to figure out once I use your credit card where I'm at. But I'm just going to tell you now—don't come after me. Give me my day. I'll be back before tomorrow night." With that, she cranked the engine.

He slammed his hand on the window. "Open up.

Don't leave."

She backed the truck out. "Be careful, Morgan. I don't want to hurt you." She didn't want to hurt him but he had sure enough hurt her. And all because of her foolish, foolish heart.

He stepped back, apparently realizing it was futile what he was doing, and she saw him staring after her in the rearview mirror. A part of her was disappointed that he didn't race for another truck and try to catch her. But, again, that was pure foolishness on her part.

CHAPTER TWENTY-ONE

Morgan watched as Amber tore out of his driveway, leaving him in the dust. His heart clenched at the thought of her being upset and on the road. But all he could think about was the look of hurt in her eyes as she had stared at him through the glass and then driven away. *How could he be so thoughtless?*

What had he been thinking? He raked a hand through his hair as he stood there, feeling about as helpless as a kid standing at his mother and father's gravesite, knowing he couldn't bring them back. His heart heavy, he stared at the diminishing plume of dust.

He had hurt Amber. His words had been callous and careless. And what she said was the truth; it was as if they had both sold their souls—he was only interested in the money. From the very beginning, he had forced himself—no, his grandfather had forced him to do this but he had signed on. And so had she, he reminded himself, feeling the pushback of all the pent-up frustrations inside him.

But had what she said been the truth? She had several reasons for signing on to this. One he had known—she felt obligated to him for having saved her life that day. He had known it and yet he had still taken advantage of it, all because he thought offering her money would fix everything. *When had he become so obsessed with money that he thought it would fix everything?*

But it was the second reason—the one she had tossed out—that slammed into him. She had been half in love with him— He thought back to different moments when he had caught her looking at him or when she had said things… *Had she fallen in love with him?*

Had he... No, he pushed the thought away. He

hadn't wanted to admit that he could have fallen in love with her. *Why?* Because of his pride? Because of his stinking control issues, not wanting his grandfather to have any part in his true love life? He stormed toward the house, his frustrations building as he let the reality of what he was thinking sink in. Would he really not let himself love when he had the chance just because he wanted to spite his granddaddy, his dead granddaddy? He stopped in his tracks and just stood there. He stared at the big house that he knew would be silent when he entered other than the puppies and Goldie.

Which reminded him that he needed to go check on them. His phone buzzed and he looked down. It was a text from Amber. He clicked to bring the messages up, hoping she had changed her mind. His adrenaline raced as he opened the message.

"Please take care of Goldie and the puppies while I'm gone."

He stared at the words. She was worried about the dog, about the puppies—worried that he wouldn't take care of them. Or worried about them and not him. That was his own fault. He thought about holding her in his arms at the dance hall while they danced and about holding her in his arms tomorrow night as they danced. What should he do? She needed time; she demanded time and per the contract, she had the right to some time. And he needed some time, too. His thoughts were crazy and bothered. *How had he let money and business take over everything? Was he just a cold-hearted shell? Was that what Granddaddy had seen in him?*

He needed to talk to his brothers.

Amber was more upset than she admitted. She wasn't sure where she was going or what she was going to do; she just knew that she had to get away. Everything was just such a lie. When she pulled into the huge ranch ten miles down the road that belonged to Talbert McCoy, Amber truly thought she had lost all of her marbles. But her mind had gone to Caroline. She needed to talk to Caroline. Caroline was hardcore in many ways but she was blunt and would tell Amber the truth. But she didn't know that Amber and Morgan had a false marriage. As she drove up to the house, she knew she was going to confide in Caroline. There was nothing in the will that said she couldn't do that. There should have been a non-disclosure if there had been a reason they wanted her to keep quiet.

She could've gone to Allie and Ginny, but they were too close to everything. They were in love with the brothers, too; they would have to be sympathetic both ways. They would encourage her. Whereas her gut told her Caroline would snap her out of this horrible daze that she was in.

She got out of the truck and saw Denton McCoy, he was a country star but pure cowboy right now, wearing chaps and a dusty shirt and a cowboy hat. He had the amazing good looks of the McCoy men. As he strode from the house the singing sensation yanked his cowboy hat off his head and slapped it across his thigh when he saw her. Though they hadn't met but once, briefly, he was memorable. But again, her heart didn't react, just the appreciation of a woman acknowledging a gorgeous man.

"Amber, how are you today? Are you okay?" He stared at her as he grew closer. "You're awfully pale."

She waved a hand dismissively. "I'm fine. Thanks

for asking, though. I just came to see Caroline. Is she home?"

He looked as though he didn't believe what she was saying as he studied her. "Yeah, she's in. She was heading to her studio when I left the kitchen. Just go on in. You'll—well, you might get lost in there. I can take you or, if you want, just go around the sidewalk and you'll see her studio. It's the glass building at the end of the pool. Actually used to be a pool room before she took it over."

"Thank you. Hope you have a good day. Looks like you're going horseback riding."

"I'm going to finish what I started. We're working cows today and I had to come in and check out some paperwork in the office. Granddaddy's in Houston today—had a big ole meeting or something, so I couldn't just call and ask him—had to actually look at it so it drug me out of what I like the most. Me and Wade—we're very much cut from the same cloth. Give us a cow to work and a horse to ride, and we're in hog heaven. Anyway, go on back there. You'll find her and maybe get some rest. You sure are pale. My cousin treating you right?"

"Everything's fine, but thanks. Talk to you later."

"I'll see you tomorrow night. I'm coming to the shindig. Gotta come and officially celebrate you and my cousin getting married. And listen to my granddad tell us it's about time one of us got married. Or all of us."

"Well, thanks. It should be a party." Her voice started to break on that word and she coughed to cover up the emotion in her throat.

"Well, I hope so because I'm really happy you married Morgan."

Why did everybody keep telling her that? They were all going to be so disappointed when the truth came out.

She strode down the sidewalk and around the huge house, until she finally saw the blue water of the pool and the pretty huge pool house. It featured white stone, lots of glass French doors and windows, with a beautiful red clay roof that matched the amazingly gorgeous red clay roof of this giant house. She could see Caroline inside. She walked along the edge of the pool and then reached the door and tapped on the window. Her stomach was rolling and her knees were weak. *Why in the world had she come and what was she about to do?*

"Amber, come on in, girl." Caroline grinned as she opened the door wide and swept her hand to indicate Amber enter the room. "This is my domain. I'm glad you're here. Come see what I'm painting."

She walked over to a big canvas. There was a picture of an amazing horse coming to life on the canvas. Amber gasped because they had talked about what a great artist Caroline was but Caroline had just pooh-poohed it all.

"They're right—you're amazing, Caroline. Oh my goodness, how beautiful this is."

"Well, thanks. It's one of the mustangs we have running around out there on our property. You know, there's a lot of acreage out here and we let some wild mustangs have certain areas of it. They're gorgeous. And contrary to what I may pretend while we're shopping, I love getting on my horse or my four-wheeler, riding out there and watching them run across the pastures. They're a beautiful group of animals. That, sadly, no one really takes serious or worries about that much—they're expendable, you know what

I mean? I hate that. Okay, I'm off my soapbox now. But, anyway, thanks. I enjoyed painting this. I'm actually thinking about trying to get in an exhibit of something for awareness—you know, mustang awareness."

"You should absolutely do that. Goodness, there's no telling what a painting like this could bring."

"I don't want, like, money for it. I'd put it in there and well, I don't know—that's a good idea. Maybe I can use it to auction off and the little bit that I make could be used for food and things. I mean, I donate quite a bit but they can always use more."

"I think whatever you decide to do would be amazing."

Caroline was very astute and she studied her. "Why are you here? You look really pale. You and my cousin have a fight?"

Bingo. Of course Caroline would know. "Well, maybe...a disagreement."

Caroline shook her head. "Nah, you don't have that shell-shock look on your face for a disagreement. Y'all had a fight and from the looks of it, it was a serious one. Come over here and sit down. Let me get you a cold drink and you tell me what that cousin of mine did to you. I'll go over there and take care of him."

She would've laughed if she weren't so sad. "No, don't go bother him. We definitely just had a disagreement. We're not seeing eye to eye on certain things."

They sat down on a couple of brightly colored chairs that overlooked the pool and she grabbed a couple of cold lemony drinks from the fridge. "Have this. Now tell me what is going on."

"I've actually run away from home for a day. I was heading to find a hotel to stay at and, well, I ended up pulling in here. I decided maybe instead of me just going and sulking that maybe I needed to talk to someone and you were my first and only thought about the person I needed to talk to."

"I am honored. You know, not a lot of people think they need to come talk to me because they think I have a little bit of a big mouth. But I don't. I'm honored. Now, I can assure you that if my cousin has done something to harm you, hurt your feelings, or whatever, I'm not going to take his side just because he's my cousin."

"And that's why I'm here. Because I need you to be open-minded. And I need clarity on what's bothering me and, well, I don't think Ginny or Allie can quite have the clarity that I need."

Caroline looked a little bit confused. "So tell me, why am I the candidate and what in the world is up?"

Could she do this? Was Caroline going to be mad? Was Morgan going to be mad when he found out she had told someone?

"See, Morgan and I—we got married to save his business."

Caroline didn't react at first. She didn't blink; she didn't budge; she didn't make any type of movement. She just stared at Amber and took in the words. After a second, she shook her head as if clearing her brain. "So you got married because he is losing his business? I know my cousin and that statement doesn't even make any sense. That is one of the best businessmen I have ever seen in my life. There's no way he could be losing his hotel and resort enterprise. So what's up?"

"It has to do with the will. The will that his grandfather J.D. left. He had to get married or he would lose his resorts and hotels."

Caroline was, for the first time that Amber had known her, speechless. And it didn't take a rocket scientist to know that Caroline McCoy was never speechless.

"You have got to be kidding me! I knew something was up when suddenly Wade and Todd both got married, although I love Allie and Ginny. I just *knew* something was up." She rubbed her forehead. "Okay, so calming myself down now. I'm not going to freak out. I really knew something was up when Morgan brought you home. Not that I have anything against you, but it's just Morgan—he's just never even acted like he was interested in anyone after the head game and tragedy of Shannon. He hardened after that, threw himself deeper into work and traveled more. Acquired more hotels and didn't have time for a girlfriend, much less a bride. But when I saw y'all, he looks at you like I've never seen him look at anyone."

"I don't know what you're seeing but it's obviously not there. That's why I'm here. I was a fool. I thought that, well, after he rescued me from the ocean in Kauai, and then found out that I worked for him, it was just a crazy time. And, well, he had never noticed me before and I had already had this huge crush on him because—well, because he *is* him. And, well, he had rescued me, so I went through with this, telling myself I wasn't going to fall for him. I wasn't going to lose my heart but that maybe he would at least notice me and this was my one shot at paradise. With him. Well, you know what I mean. I mean, honestly, think about it—again, I'm a fool but I mean it was all so coincidental. Mrs. Beasley got me there; Mrs. Beasley knew about the plan. And then me walking out there and nearly drowning—that was completely coincidental, and then him being there on that cliff and seeing me and rescuing me—well, it's the thing TV dreams are made of.

"I guess I let my foolish self get caught up in that and it's all a fairy tale. Just so wrong and fake, and that's exactly what this is—a fake marriage. It's legal but it's fake on an emotional level and on a heart-to-heart level. Anyway, I need advice. I've got to make it through the next month and a few days. And tomorrow night…it's just all such a lie and I don't know if I can do it. But I'm not worried about me. I mean, I should have never signed on this with a money deal. I don't have to have the money. I can work just like I've always done, but if I walk out on him, I can't do that. I mean, he'll lose everything that means something to him. He'll lose his resorts and it will be my fault because I gave him my word, my vow that I would be here."

Caroline studied her, her expression very serious. "Girlfriend, I know exactly what we're going to do. You are going to stay here tonight. And you're about my size, so we're going to get you ready for the show tomorrow night. I have a plan. And if my cousin is too stupid and stubborn to miss out on the best thing that has ever happened to him, then I just can't help him. But if he needs a wakeup call, then, honey, we are going to give him exactly what he needs. You stick with me. We'll have that man drooling. Oh, yeah, this is going to be fun."

* * *

Morgan about went crazy the rest of the afternoon, worrying about Amber. He kept looking at his phone; he kept texting her, telling her to let him know where she was and that she was safe. And to come home. That they would work this out. That everything would be fine. But she didn't respond. And he was worried sick. Finally, about midnight, he got a text from her. But all it said was: "I'm safe. I'll see you tomorrow at the party."

At the party? She wasn't going to come home until the party? He texted back furiously. "Call me. I'll call...you answer the phone." He dialed the number but she didn't answer. He texted again: "Listen to me. We need to talk before the party. We have to talk."

He waited and finally the text came through: "There's nothing to talk about. I'll see you at the party. Don't call. I'm not going to answer and don't text back. I'm safe."

He stared at the screen. *Why was she doing this?* He was not used to someone bucking him. Horses bucked; people did not buck him. Needless to say, he didn't sleep well. He drifted off and he woke up and felt worse than he did when he didn't sleep.

He paced; he went into the bedroom that was his that she had been using and he stared at all of her stuff. It felt lonely and it didn't even seem like his room anymore. There were remembrances of her everywhere he walked. He opened the closet and looked at her clothes. They just hung there. He found himself fingering them, wishing she were in them…wishing she were here. He walked into the bathroom. Her brush lay on the counter. Everything was nice and neat. He picked up her brush. Fingered the little bit of hair that was stuck in it and walked back into the bedroom. He sat on the edge of the bed that was neatly made and stared around the room, feeling about as lost as he had ever felt.

He made it through the night and was making coffee the next morning, not happy. He paced the kitchen as he waited on the coffeemaker to finish making his coffee. When it was done, he grabbed the mug and poured the coffee too quickly into the mug, sloshing it everywhere. He snatched the cup off the counter and mopped up the mess. Then, taking his coffee, he strode out onto the deck and stared grimly at the horizon. It was a new day. *What a joke.*

His eyes were gritty, his stomach churned, and he wondered where Amber was. *Had she slept okay? Was she safe?* He knew that she had his credit card, so he knew she could afford to get a room and she had her own cards. He knew she had money, so that wasn't the problem. The problem was he just didn't know where she was and he needed to see her. He had never needed to see anyone so badly in all of his life. The very thought slammed into him and his heart crashed against his chest as if it were trying to break loose.

He missed his parents, he missed his granddaddy despite their differences, but he had never felt the raw, churning and gut-wrenching explosion of emotion that held him tightly wound all night and now. He had hurt Amber and he needed to see her. He needed to apologize to her. He needed to make this right. *But how could he do that?* He felt trapped. As he took a drink of the hot coffee, letting it burn all the way down to his gut, he let his pride go.

CHAPTER TWENTY-TWO

Wade, Todd, and his cousins Ash and Denton all stood in a circle, talking, as they waited for Amber to arrive. He had assured them, despite not being certain that she would show up, that she would be here. He had joked that women had to primp and she was spending extra time for this special occasion. He had no idea what she was doing but that's all he had for them. He watched out of the corner of his eye as Allie and Ginny chattered among themselves, shooting him glances every once in a while that he refused to meet their gaze on.

If they knew what was going on, they hadn't said

anything to him. He had asked them whether they had talked to Amber, hoping that if they had talked to her and knew what was going on that they would let on, but it was the only way he could ask it without alerting them that he hadn't talked to her. But both of them told him that no, they hadn't talked to her. He wasn't sure whether he believed them or not but that's all he said.

Penny, grinning, came up. "So I guess your bride's going to make a grand entrance. I kind of like that. I'll get to see all the excitement on your face when she walks in like Cinderella, all beautiful and gorgeous."

He stared at Penny, dumbfounded.

Penny knew exactly what this marriage was made of and yet she was pretending that it was true love that had brought them together. He wasn't sure when Penny had ever become such a great actress but obviously she was because she didn't even act as though she were leading people on. It was the craziest thing he ever saw. "Yeah, Penny, I guess that's what she's going to do. I'll be glad when she gets here."

"I could tell by the look on your face that you'll be glad when she gets here. Morgan McCoy, you look like a lovesick puppy. I never thought I'd see the day when you had that look on your face." Penny patted his arm. "Your granddaddy would be proud."

He stared at her, not at all sure what she was talking about.

"She does have a point." Denton grinned. "I saw her the other day—I guess yesterday—and she looked kind of pale but she said she was fine. You look a little bit pale yourself right now."

His gaze cut to his cousin. "You saw her yesterday?"

"Yeah, at the house. She came by to see Caroline."

"Oh, well, did Caroline say anything about why she came by?"

"I don't know. You know, I don't live at the house. I had just gone in there to look at something for Granddaddy, so I never talked to her again or Caroline. I was working cattle and then went home."

His mind raced. *Had she gone to see Caroline and then gone from there? Or was she with his cousin now?* He had half hoped she was with Caroline; at least he'd know she was safe and that someone knew where she was.

"Are you okay, Morgan?" Wade asked.

"Yeah, you do look really worried." Todd stared at him intently. "Have you seen Amber today?"

"No, I haven't seen her today. Look, guys, she left yesterday." He glanced at his brothers because they knew good and well that his cousins didn't know the truth. But at this point, who in the heck cared. "Look," he said to Ash and Denton. Beck had gotten caught in Canada when a storm delayed flights. "This whole thing is a lie—a joke. Or it was. I don't know what to call it but for y'all, it's a lie. Your granddaddy and Penny and me and Todd and Wade all know the truth and y'all might as well know it too. Granddaddy gave us ultimatums—we had to marry within three months, each one after the other, and stay married for three months or we lose everything. I lose the resorts and the hotels. And, you know, I've been angry at Granddaddy about it but mostly right now, I'm angry at myself because I fell for this and I don't even care anymore. But y'all should know that I don't know if Amber's going to come back or not. Yeah, we were upset. I upset her yesterday because like an idiot, I said basically we'd had an agreement, that it was about money and that I resented it because Granddaddy had forced me into getting married."

Ash and Denton both looked totally mind-boggled.

Ash was the first to speak. "This is fake? Like, a fake marriage?"

"Yeah, Todd and Wade's were too but they got their happily-ever-afters, like some romantic movie or something. And, well, then it was my turn. And I hate to say it, but I have really made a big stupid mess of everything."

"Morgan, are you okay?" Wade asked again. "Because I'm telling you, brother, the way you're acting, it's not like a guy who thinks this is all about money."

Talbert walked up about that time. "Morgan, I just want to come by and congratulate you. You've got a beautiful bride there. I'll tell you what, we all heard about Wade and Allie expecting and I just want to say your granddaddy is doing a jig up in heaven right now, along with your mom and dad."

He eyed Ash and Denton. "Boys, I think it's about time y'all set your caps on getting married. I've got a lot of money riding on the issue right now. And I think we're going to have us a little Texas tough talk after tonight. 'Cuz you know what, I've got a hankering for a great-grandbaby, too, and none of y'all are getting any younger. I'm getting a whole lot older, so we're going to have to settle this."

Everybody looked at Talbert as if he were losing it. Morgan didn't even care. He felt for his cousins but he could see the writing on the wall. It was catching—all this was catching. All he wanted was away from it all and Amber. He had to talk to Amber.

"Uncle Talbert, what you're talking about, I wouldn't wish on anybody. I'd think long and hard about that—" His words ended abruptly as he saw movement at the door and Caroline walked in and shot him a look straight across the room that was like daggers. Then she gave him that little smirk of hers like when they were kids and she had gone and tattled on everybody just to see them get in trouble.

And then she looked back at the door and in walked Amber.

She was stunning. She wore a black dress that clung to her beautiful figure and was off the shoulders. It had Caroline's style written all over it but it looked good on Amber. His heart hammered and his pulse felt faint, it raced so fast. It seemed as if everybody between him and Amber parted and there was only the wide expanse of emptiness between them. He didn't want emptiness between them. As he looked at her, she could've been standing there in rags and he would've felt the same way. He didn't want emptiness between them; he didn't want anything between them. He took a step forward and walked steadily and purposefully toward her.

All of his life, he knew what he wanted. And he went after it with the single-mindedness and the control of a man who knew how to get what he wanted. And until yesterday, until Amber had walked away from him, he had never let emotion get in the way of a deal. And yet, that was all this was now with Amber—emotion. He loved her.

She stood there and he could see her hands tremble as they were clasped at her abdomen. Her eyes were trying to be emotionless but they were so full of emotion that he felt for her. When he reached her, he held his hand out to her. The music played behind them, as if Penny had told the orchestra to start.

"May I have this dance?" he asked, willing her to slip her hand into his. The old Clint Black and Lisa

Hartman song "When I Said I Do" played; the heartfelt country song of the great singer and his bride throbbed between them and he had never felt something so strong in all of his life as he did now, as he willed her to take his hand.

"When I said I do, I meant it," he said softly. Her eyes widened as he wiggled his fingers, drawing her attention. He swallowed the lump in his throat as he watched her gaze drop to his hand and then swing back up to his. The pulse beat in the artery at her neck, and her eyes filled with tears. And then her hand slid into his.

Elation filled him and he tugged her gently toward him, swept her into his arms and then swept her out onto the dancefloor, swaying with her to the music. As Clint Black sang his heart out to the love of his life, Morgan felt every piece of his life click into place.

He breathed her scent in, felt her body swaying with his. He gazed into her sweet, beautiful eyes. He held her close and he gently brushed the tear off her cheek. "When I said I do, I didn't know how much I meant it until now, until yesterday when you drove out of my life. All night, I was terrified that I had lost you—that I had been such a fool. And all the time you were thinking you were the fool. You weren't. I don't care how we started. I don't care about the money. I don't care about if it was my granddaddy. All I care about is that you are my wife and you'll stay my wife."

"You don't really mean that."

"Oh, but I do, darlin'. I mean it with every fiber of my being. I can't make you stay married to me but I'm going to live the rest of my life trying to get you back if you leave me. I don't care if I lose everything. All that matters to me right now is you and that you're mine forever. I want to build a life with you. I want to have however many kids you want to have. I want to do whatever you want to do. If you want to work with me in the business, that's fine. Or if we want to give the business up, I don't care. I realized last night that without you in my life, I don't have anything. I lost my mom and dad when I was young and I lost my granddad. And as much as I loved them, even though me and my granddaddy had that contentiousness between us, losing you was devastating. I love you."

He stopped dancing. She trembled in his arms and she wasn't saying anything. Tears streamed down her face, too many for him to stop with his fingers. He cupped her face in his hands and he slowly kissed her tears from her cheeks. He kissed one cheek then he kissed the other; then he kissed one eye and then the other eyelid as she had closed her eyes. "Tell me you love me or what I have to do to make this right."

"I love you, Morgan, and you've made it right. I just can't believe it's true."

His whole world clicked into place. He picked her up in his arms; she gasped and her arms went around his neck. As the song finished, he twirled them around, holding her close. "I can't believe you came back to me."

She laughed and placed her forehead to his as he twirled them around and people clapped. "Oh, Morgan, I never really left. You've had my heart—always."

"And that makes me the happiest man in the world." And then he brought them to a standstill and lowered his lips to hers.

Check out the next book in the McCoy Billionaire Brothers series, HER BILLIONAIRE COWBOY'S SECRET BABY SURPRISE

About the Author

Hope Moore is the pen name of an award-winning author who lives deep in the heart of Texas surrounded by Christian cowboys who give her inspiration for all of her inspirational sweet romances. She loves writing clean & wholesome, swoon worthy romances for all of her fans to enjoy and share with everyone. Her heartwarming, feel good romances are full of humor and heart, and gorgeous cowboys and heroes to love. And the spunky women they fall in love with and live happily-ever-after.

When she isn't writing, she's trying very hard not to cook, since she could live on peanut butter sandwiches, shredded wheat, coffee...and cheesecake why should she cook? She loves writing though and creating new stories is her passion. Though she does love shoes, she's admitted she has an addiction and tries really hard to stay out of shoe stores. She, however, is not addicted to social media and chooses to write instead of surf FB - but she LOVES her readers so she's working on a free novella just for you and if you sign up for her newsletter she will send it to you as soon as its ready! You'll also receive snippets of her adventures, along with special deals, sneak peaks of soon-to-be released books and of course any sales she might be having.

She promises she will not spam you, she hates to be spammed also, so she wouldn't dare do that to people she's crazy about (that means YOU). You can unsubscribe at any time.

Sign up for my newsletter:
www.subscribepage.com/hopemooresignup

I can't wait to hear from you.

Hope Moore~
Always hoping for more love, laughter and reading for you every day of your life!

Made in the USA
Las Vegas, NV
17 February 2021